TWO DEATH TALES

DOLMEN TEXTS 2

DOLMEN TEXTS 2

Set in Baskerville type and printed in the Republic of Ireland
by Cahill Printers Limited for the publishers,
The Dolmen Press Limited, Mountrath, Portlaoise, Ireland.
North America Humanities Press Inc.,
Atlantic Highlands, N.J. 07716, U.S.A.

Designed by Liam Miller

First published 1981

BRITISH LIBRARY CATALOGUING IN PUBLICATION DATA

Two death tales from the Ulster Cycle —
    (Dolmen texts; 2).
    I. Tymoczko, Maria   II. Death of Cu Roi
    III. Death of CuChulainn
    398.2'2'09415   GR153.5

ISBN 0 85105 342 4 The Dolmen Press
     0 391 02136 2 Humanities Press

TWO DEATH TALES FROM THE ULSTER
CYCLE: THE DEATH OF CU ROI AND THE
DEATH OF CU CHULAINN TRANSLATED
BY MARIA TYMOCZKO FROM THE IRISH

DUBLIN: THE DOLMEN PRESS
NORTH AMERICA: HUMANITIES PRESS INC.

To Susan
who listened to many tales from me
while these translations were brought forth
and always wanted to hear more.

The preparation of this volume was made possible by a grant from the Translations Program of the National Endowment for the Humanities, an independent federal agency of the United States of America.

CONTENTS

FOREWORD

SOME PEOPLE MAY consider the publication of these translations premature: a translation should only be undertaken after a text has been adequately established, they will say. Until there is a critical edition, for example, discretion would counsel against translation. This is no doubt true. Because no definitive edition exists for either text in this book, the translations here are necessarily tentative.

Were these stories strictly of interest to scholars, I would be swayed by such scholarly concerns. But three generations of scholarship have failed to produce adequate editions of these texts. Moreover, the problems posed by the language of the originals are so massive that conceivably we could wait another long while until editions would appear and translations fully grounded in received texts could be undertaken.

Ultimately I decided to let these translations be published because I believe these tales do not belong simply to scholars of whom I am one. They belong to the Irish people and to those everywhere who are interested in Irish tradition and impatient to know as much as they can now.

What errors are to be found in this book will be overshadowed, I trust, by the larger movement of the stories and the overall fidelity to the beautiful but difficult poetry in the tales. I can only hope that these translations will help pave the way for critical editions of the texts and, later, for better translations. In the meantime this purpose has motivated me: to return these works as a gift to a culture which has given me so much.

MARIA FLEMING TYMOCZKO
Northampton, Massachusetts
April, 1980

INTRODUCTION

WE ARE ACCUSTOMED to seeing CuChulainn as the
impetuous and victorious hero of the Ulstermen. In *The
Death of CuRoi* and *The Death of CuChulainn* he is
alternately neither daring nor victorious. Thus, these stories
challenge our fundamental predispositions towards early
Irish heroism and hero tale. It is a challenge that must be
faced squarely, for the versions of the tales translated here
are among the oldest Irish saga texts. The perspectives they
offer go back to the roots of Irish tradition and serve as
correctives to modern interpretation.

The savage story of the death of CuRoi at the hands of
CuChulainn and Blathnait is particularly important for our
understanding of the Ulster Cycle and the roles of
CuChulainn and CuRoi. It was a favourite tale in early
Ireland, if we are to judge from the number of different
versions that have survived in the manuscripts. In *The
Death of CuRoi* CuChulainn is far from invincible; in fact,
CuRoi makes rather short work of him. CuChulainn's
victory when it comes is hardly a triumph; it is born of
conspiracy and treachery and unequal combat.
CuChulainn is not really the hero of this story at all;
paradoxically, CuRoi is.

The emotional centre of the saga is a long praise poem to
CuRoi, *Amra ConRói*, 'The Eulogy of CuRoi'. It is true
that the story tells of CuRoi's downfall, but it does not
narrate his defeat. The treachery that destroys him parallels
other uncontrollable forces that have the power to ensnare
great heroes: the gods, magic or supernatural powers, the
violation of tabus and *geasa,* and fate. CuRoi is caught up in
a web of treachery; and it is the treachery itself, not
CuChulainn, that destroys him. CuChulainn as a character is
merely part of a greater destructive vortex. Thus, CuRoi
stands in the long line of heroes who are destroyed, but
never simply defeated.

While the story of CuChulainn's own death is similar to
The Death of CuRoi, it is fate and supernatural forces more
than treachery that engulf him. Since CuChulainn is an
extraordinary hero, he could be expected to meet with an
extraordinary death. So it is that he is not merely cut down

11

on the field of battle or defeated by a more glorious hand. His death is highlighted by familiar elements reserved for the greatest heroes: he is caught by conflicting demands of his *geasa* and his honour; he dies isolated from his king and comrades at the hands of overwhelming forces; his death is plotted and planned; he is brought down by sorcery and occult powers; his death is presaged by portents and prophecy. Ultimately CuChulainn may be killed by his own weapons, but like CuRoi he dies in a defiant, undefeated posture. These themes re-echo in early heroic literature from *The Destruction of DaDerga's Hostel* and *The Song of Roland* to the Icelandic sagas.

In many ways CuChulainn's death is the climax of his career. The story presupposes a great deal. It alludes to CuChulainn's birth, his childhood and training in arms, as well as his mature deeds and great exploits. In particular, the story presupposes knowledge of those he killed, for in *The Death of CuChulainn* the children of his slain opponents come to avenge their fathers. Because the tale is dependent on so many other stories about CuChulainn, in a sense it is derivative. We see this especially in the relation of the tale to *Táin Bó Cúailnge*, 'The Cattle-raid of Cuailnge'; the plot of *The Death of CuChulainn* is modelled rather closely on that longer narrative.

A curious aspect of *The Death of CuChulainn* is its dual perspective. As the narrative shifts back and forth from CuChulainn and Ulster to CuChulainn's enemies and their army, CuChulainn's opponents do not appear uniformly bad or ignoble or ridiculous. Because both CuRoi's son Lugaid and Erc, son of Coirpre, are treated with a certain dignity or grandeur, they appeal to the audience. This viewpoint may have something to do with CuChulainn's role in *The Death of CuRoi* and the tone of that story. CuChulainn's death when it comes is not altogether undeserved — in the end treachery brings its own reward.

The Death of CuChulainn has a solemn and stately tone. As in a processional or pageant, the events here have a ritualistic quality. The action proceeds through a series of gestures and pronouncements, and we are given a kaleidoscope of static images more than a continuous flow of events linked by causality. The use of CuChulainn's solemn statements to mark off the stages of his journey to death

12

gives the story an inconographic dimension; in some ways it is reminiscent of the passion of Christ.

Irish narrative, however, is rarely totally tragic; it is generally characterized by a mixture of tones. The greatest tragedies can be marked by farce, and comedy has its own cutting edge. Even in the story of CuChulainn's death, the narrator finds humour irresistible. The result is a tongue-in-cheek presentation of CuChulainn's encounters with three pairs of fighting men. Thus, humour is used as a foil in incidents central to the tragedy. Two moods are entwined here as elsewhere in Irish tradition.

In many ways, then, these two death tales from the Ulster cycle highlight anomalous yet crucial features of Irish hero tale. We see from the praise of CuRoi in *The Eulogy of CuRoi* and from the entire tone of *The Death of CuRoi*, that CuChulainn was not the only beloved hero in the Ulster cycle, nor perhaps always the primary one. We are reminded that CuChulainn was not faultless or invincible, or even always dignified — an observation that also can be made of CuRoi and perhaps of all heroes. That CuRoi and CuChulainn can be louse-ridden and dung-smeared, that they have domestic obligations, that they can be laughed at, and yet are heroes nonetheless, is worth pondering. We have heard such messages in our time, but these stories show that the idea is not new.

Neither CuRoi nor CuChulainn is faultless, and their fates become intertwined because of their faults. It is CuRoi's absolute humiliation of CuChulainn — his unwillingness even to talk with his enemy — that leads to CuChulainn's uncompromising vengeance and CuRoi's death. But CuChulainn is willing to exact vengeance by any means, even treachery — hardly an honourable course. His own death is the ultimate result. It is no accident that CuRoi's son Lugaid throws the mortal cast at CuChulainn and is the one to behead CuChulainn and carry off the spoils. Of course, in a blood feud no one wins — least of all Lugaid in *The Death of CuChulainn*. To point out the heroes' faults, the ways in which they contribute to their own demise, and the destructiveness of feuding is not to suggest that these are simple moral tales. It is to say, however, that heroic death is not as arbitrary, or as unsullied, or as tragic as we would sometimes have it.

13

Finally, it is significant that neither death tale ends with the hero's death. In both there is a coda of vengeance and fighting. Though one hero dies, others rise to fill his place. Because the struggle continues beyond the death of either hero, these death tales paradoxically affirm the continuity of life. It is fitting in this context that *The Death of CuChulainn* ends with both lament and prophecy. The old age passes away in grief, perhaps, only to inaugurate the next.[1]

Two early forms of *The Death of CuChulainn* are extant. A fifteenth-century version of the tale has survived in many modern manuscripts where it is generally entitled *Brislech Mór Maige Muirtheimne*, 'The Great Defeat on Muirtheimne Plain', and *Dergruathar Chonaill Chernaig*, 'Conall Cernach's Red Rampage'. This widely known version of the story has been edited, translated and retold in modern form. In general the fifteenth-century version of the tale is the immediate ancestor of modern tradition. In its modern forms the story has had great impact on Irish culture — on Pearse, on Yeats, and daily on those who enter the GPO.

In the Middle Irish tale lists the earliest versions of the story are called *Aided ConCulainn*, 'The Death of CuChulainn'. Only one text survives from the pre-Norman period, the version in the Book of Leinster (LL), 119a-123b. A few sentences from the same version survive in a second manuscript, Trinity College H.3.18 (ca. 1500), where they are used to illustrate lexical points. In this second manuscript the passages are labelled 'In Brislech co sin'. On this basis, the LL text, like the fifteenth-century version, has been called *Brislech Mór Maige Muirtheimne*.

The LL text represents an ancestor of all the later versions of CuChulainn's death. It is both more simple and more complex than the fifteenth-century version. The account of CuChulainn's death is brief and stark, but the form is rich and varied. Passages of *rosc* — the cryptic, dense, alliterative, visionary poetry representing the earliest and most archaic tradition of poetry in Ireland — constitute almost half the text.

Pokorny has dated the tale as a whole to the mid eighth century at the latest; this is earlier than the Wurzburg glosses, and he calls it one of the earliest saga texts we possess.[2] The poetry may be even older than the prose. Both because of the early date of the tale and the late assignment of the title *Brislech Mór* to this version, I think we are justified in identifying it with the story represented in the saga lists as *Aided ConCulainn*, 'The Death of CuChulainn'.[3]

The LL text of *The Death of CuChulainn* has never before been translated in its entirety. In 1877 Whitley Stokes translated excerpts into English, and later in 1892 he contributed to a translation into French of all the prose and a small amount of the poetry. Two subsequent French translations of the prose have appeared, but no translator has attempted the entire text until now. The passages of *rosc* have presented the barrier to translation: the language in the passages is archaic and deliberately cryptic, and there is no second manuscript to help resolve obscure readings. The text of these poems has also suffered the vagaries of time. The passages were passed on by copyists who often did not understand the forms in them, or, worse yet, thought they did and 'modernized' the spellings. Once the cadenced metres ceased to be commonly used, the *roscada* became still more vulnerable. Often they were not recognized as poetry, and their grammar was regularized to prose standards.

Though the translation of many lines continues to remain difficult and at times a matter of conjecture, recent scholarship offers tools to aid in the interpretation of the *roscada*. In 1963 Calvert Watkins ('Indo-European Metrics and Archaic Irish Verse', *Celtica* 6, 194-249), showed that many similar passages are poetry, and he offered a theory of their metrical principles. This and more recent work on archaic poetry, particularly that of James Carney, have made it possible to establish the metrics of the *roscada* in this saga. In many cases an interpretation of the sense of the lines followed only from the metrical guidelines: in poetry meaning and metre are interdependent.

The opening paragraphs of the LL text of *The Death of CuChulainn* are missing because of a lacuna in the manuscript. It is likely that only a single leaf has been lost, in which case some 175 lines of text or 1,750 words are missing.[4] Fortunately a portion of the lost material (125 words) has been preserved in the brief extracts in Trinity

15

College H.3.18. The translation of *The Death of CuChulainn* begins with a summary of the main lines of the lost opening as it can be reconstructed on the basis of material preserved in Trinity College II.3.18 and the circumstances indicated in the rest of the text.

Though no full version of *The Death of CuRoi* was recorded in the twelfth-century manuscripts that contain most of the Ulster cycle, three early versions are found in later manuscripts. British Museum Egerton 88 may contain the oldest version of *The Death of CuRoi*; Thurneysen has dated it to the eighth or ninth century.[5] The tale is short, but it gives a rather clear account of the battle at CuRoi's fort. In this early version CuRoi is invulnerable because he has an external soul which is carefully concealed in an apple inside a salmon which surfaces only once every seven years. Only when CuRoi's wife learns his secret and divulges it to CuChulainn, can he fall. This plot follows the lines of a common folktale, 'The Ogre's Heart in the Egg'.

A second version of *The Death of CuRoi* is found in a fifteenth-century manuscript, Bodleian Laud 610. Laud 610 is primarily a compendium of poetry pertaining to the death of CuRoi, including the whole of *Brinna Ferchertne*, 'Ferchertne's Dream-Vision' (see below, p. 17). The poetry in this account is given a prose context, but the prose elements are quite brief. Nevertheless, it is clear that the narrative follows the main lines of the story as it is translated below, and also that Laud 610 represents an independent telling of the story rather than a summary of the longest early version.[6]

The third and longest version of *The Death of CuRoi* is found in the fourteenth-century Yellow Book of Lecan (YBL). The language of this text is no earlier than the tenth century, and may be as late as the twelfth century.[7] Part of this version is also found in Egerton 88. The YBL version is flawed. It has been manipulated by scribes, and it is full of learned asides — etymologies, added quatrains, and glosses to explain words or passages. It is a version of the story that is apparently far removed from immediate oral transcription; the fossilized glosses incorporated into the text frequently give a sense of redundancy and speak of a relatively long manuscript tradition. Despite all these defects, I have

16

chosen YBL as the basis for my translation because the text has glories, too. It is the longest and fullest early version of CuRoi's death. More important, it contains the most powerful poem pertaining to the death of CuRoi, *Amra Conrói*, 'The Eulogy of CuRoi'.

Like the more famous *Amra Choluim Chille*, 'The Eulogy of St. Columba', this poem is in the cadenced metres of the *roscada* in *The Death of CuChulainn*. It is characteristic of such poetry that the stanzas are of irregular length and that the only poetic ornaments are alliteration and end cadence. *The Eulogy of CuRoi* is dense and cryptic. Those are the qualities that make it at once powerful and hard to translate. At the latest *The Eulogy of CuRoi* was written down by the first decades of the eighth century.[8] Like the LL version of *The Death of CuChulainn*, then, this poem carries us back to the oldest layer of written Irish tales.

The YBL version of *The Death of CuRoi* is concerned with topography. The teller had real places in mind when he narrated the story. CuRoi's fort is on the Dingle Peninsula; the great hillfort near Camp in the Slieve Mish Mountains is still called Caherconree, 'CuRoi's fort'. Standing 2,050 feet above the sea, it may be the highest hillfort in Ireland. Similarly, other place names mentioned in the story had specific referents: Srub Brain (Raven's Beak), Finnglais (White Stream), Cenn Bera, Airgetglenn. The action of the story gives names to a real landscape that may have been familiar to the teller's audience.

In addition to the saga versions of *The Death of CuRoi*, other early material associated with the story has survived. Topographical articles and poems about Finnglais appear in the Book of Leinster, the Book of Ballymote, the Book of Lecan, Trinity College H.3.3, and the Rennes *dindshenchas*; these articles essentially give brief summaries of the tale translated here. In addition there are *dindshenchas* articles on Srub Brain in the same five manuscripts. *Amra ConRói* also appears as an independent piece in Trinity College H.3.18 where it is fully glossed.

Finally, there is an interesting tenth-century poem about the death of CuRoi entitled *Brinna Ferchertne*, 'Ferchertne's Dream-Vision'.[9] This poem is in the later syllabic metres; it is in rimed quatrains. The poem has been preserved as part of the Laud 610 version of *The Death of CuRoi* (see above, p. 16). *Ferchertne's Dream-Vision* is ostensibly Ferchertne's prophetic dream utterance about the death of CuRoi; stanzas at the beginning and at the end of the poem begin with the visionary formula *at-chíu*, 'I see'. The body of the poem is a series of narrative quatrains in the past tense telling the events of CuRoi's death. Since the use of the past tense is not unusual in prophecy or visionary utterance, and since straight narrative poetry is extremely rare in early Irish literature, it is likely that the poem forms a unity; the stanzas beginning with the visionary formula should not be separated from the stanzas in the narrative past tense.[10] The poetry in *Ferchertne's Dream-Vision* is rather flat and undistinguished, but it tells the story clearly. Quatrains from this poem are quoted in the YBL version of the saga.

The author or teller who is responsible for the YBL text of *The Death of CuRoi* knew the mass of oral and written tradition about CuRoi's death. He included or alluded to a good deal: a simple oral version (similar to Laud 610) seems to provide the framework for the story, but it is filled out with topographical material including allusions to the stories about Srub Brain and Finnglais, narrative quatrains from *Ferchertne's Dream-Vision*, and the whole of *The Eulogy of CuRoi*. The central narrative about the battle is based on *Ferchertne's Dream-Vision*; quatrains from the poem are introduced briefly with a prose sentence or two. This section of the tale may have replaced a more direct and simple prose account of the battle. It is difficult to say whether all these materials were brought together in an oral version or whether they are the work of a lettered scholar. This text may be important as we come to understand more clearly the process by which early tales were recorded from oral tradition and the way they developed in the early manuscript tradition.

These translations were begun in 1975 as part of a series of seminars in Advanced Old Irish at the University of Massachusetts, Amherst. The classes were offered as part of the Five-College Irish Studies program. I am indebted to Lisa Bitel, Anne Marie Casey, Mary Dowd, Mary McGarry, and Susan Rodley for their intelligent and preserving efforts with the Old Irish texts and to Warren Anderson, David R. Clark, Alison Knowles, Leone Stein, Harold Skulsky, and Thomas Tymoczko for their comments on the translations. I would also like to thank Thomas Kinsella and Thomas Tymoczko for their insights on translation theory, and I am grateful to Proinsias MacCana for reviewing the final text and sparing me many errors. Any problems that remain are, of course, my responsibility. Finally, my special thanks to Paul Dixey who in the course of working on *The Death of CuChulainn* has evolved from student to colleague.

A NOTE ON THE TRANSLATION

THIS IS AN ATTEMPT to produce translations that will be interesting to general readers and useful to scholars at the same time. Thus, the translations are as literal as contemporary English usage permits. They are line-by-line translations of the manuscripts as they have come down to us; occasionally clauses are inverted, but other departures from the order of the originals are indicated in the notes. The translation of *The Death of CuChulainn* could be used to elucidate the diplomatic edition of the story in the manner of a facing translation.

Since a translation can never capture all the features of the original, translators must make choices. I have chosen here to focus on the content of the tales, and I have attempted to avoid adding or omitting anything. When possible I have tried to capture the tone of the original — to preserve the starkness, the humour, the simplicity or the ornateness of Old Irish style in its various guises.

There is no attempt to reproduce features of early Irish syntax and phraseology. Instead, functional equivalents in current English have been used. Tense and voice have been normalized to modern English usage. This is particularly true, in prophetic passages where the original uses a variety of tenses including the past tense which is appropriate to visionary certainty. In the translations prophecy is given primarily in the future tense.

In general any given Irish word is translated consistently with the same English equivalent. Thus, when the vocabulary of the original is repetitious, so is the translation. Such repetition is characteristic of oral style. The repertory of verbs in the translations is to some extent larger than that of the originals. This lexical pungency compensates somewhat for the loss of emphasis on the verb inherent in normal Irish word order where the verb stands at the head of the clause and also implicit in constructions involving impersonal passives; these constructions are necessarily forgone when one transposes Irish into English syntax.

All languages are composed of sub-classes of language, including technical vocabularies. Old Irish is no exception, and on occasion this has affected the translation. In *The*

Death of CuChulainn, for example, CuChulainn's prophecies at times incorporate a great number of Christian religious terms. I have attempted to indicate that change in language variety by using words with a Biblical or a liturgical ring in the translation.

The translations of the passages of *rosc* were the most difficult part of the work and remain the least satisfactory. Many readings continue to be doubtful at best. Though emendation was a last recourse, it was at times necessary in order to arrive at a text that would yield an acceptable translation. The textual notes that accompany this work are only minimal. It is my hope to provide a fuller discussion of the textual problems in a future edition of the *roscada*.

The 'stepped form' of passages of poetry in the translations represents an attempt to capture some features of the original metrics in the passages of *rosc*. In most *roscada*, each line is composed of two short elements — a colon that can vary in its syllabic count though the number of stressed syllables may be fixed, and a final cadence typically three syllables long. Alliteration is the only ornament. The stepped form in the translation preserves this division into two cola, though the final cadence is not maintained. In the original the syntactical relations of the cola are often ambiguous, and I have refrained from imposing false clarity through grammatical devices or punctuation.

These translations were undertaken, in part, to supplement the selection of tales translated by Thomas Kinsella in *The Táin*. Hence, in preparing the notes I have occasionally referred to that volume rather than summarize material contained there. I have also at times followed Kinsella's lead in translating specific words, in the treatment of formulas, and in the presentation of proper nouns. Thus, for example, I have translated *ces* by 'pangs' as he does in *The Táin*. This consistency will be useful to readers who have used Kinsella's collection. Time and again Kinsella's translations have offered guidance and inspiration; *The Táin* has been a touchstone for me, and I am pleased to be able to acknowledge my indebtedness to that work.

THE DEATH OF CU ROI

'What reason did the men of Ulster have to kill CuRoi mac Dairi? '[1]

'THAT IS EASY. It was on account of that weasel Blathnait, stammering Menn's daughter, who was carried off from the siege of Falga's men, and on account of Iuchna's three red-spotted cows, and on account of the three ear-delighting fellows.'[2]

They were little birds on the cows' ears—Iuchna's red-spotted cows. A cauldron was carried off with the cows. It was their 'calf'. Thirty oxen would fit in the cauldron, and the cows milked it full whenever the birds sang to them. CuChulainn spoke of it in *The Phantom Chariot:*[3]

> 'In the fort was a cauldron
> the calf of the three cows.
> Thirty oxen in its maw
> was what it could hold.
>
> It was a pleasing challenge:
> they gathered round
> they did not go
> until they left it full.
>
> Great gold and silver
> was in it — a good hoard.
> Myself I took that cauldron
> and the king's daughter.'

Now CuRoi mac Dairi went with the men of

Ulster to the siege, and they did not recognize him. They called him 'the man in the cream-coloured cloak'.

Conchobor inquired about each head brought from the fort: 'Who killed that man?'

'Me, and the man in the cream-coloured cloak,' each man said in turn.

But when it was time to divide the spoils, they did not make a share for CuRoi. So, they were not just to him. He sped in among the cows, and he herded them together before him. He tied the birds in his belt, and he took the woman under one of his arms. They went off with the cauldron on his shoulder. None of the Ulstermen managed to speak to him but CuChulainn alone. CuRoi turned on him and pushed him into the earth up to his arm-pits. He sheared him bald with his sword and dumped the cows' dung on his head. CuRoi went from them then and reached his house.

After that CuChulainn kept away from the men of Ulster for a whole year. Then one day, when he was at Boirche's Peaks, he saw a big flock of black birds coming toward him across the open sea. He killed one of the birds immediately. After that he killed a bird from the flock in each district [they flew over] till he reached Srub Brain in western Ireland. From the head of the black bird he took there it is called Srub Brain, Raven's Beak. This is how he happened to come westward to the hillfort of CuRoi. He knew then it was CuRoi who had shamed him.[4]

He spoke with the woman, for he had loved her even before she was brought over the sea. She was the daughter of Iuchna, king of the men of Falga (so called because it was a breakwater, *fál*, in the islands of the sea, *gó*.)[5] He arranged to meet her again in the west on Samain night.

A province of Ireland set out to go with Cu-Chulainn then. That day she gave CuRoi advice provided by CuChulainn — CuRoi should make a splendid rampart for his hillfort from every standing-stone in Ireland, whether erect or toppled. The Clan Dedad roused themselves on that very day to make the stronghold, so there was no one but himself in his hillfort. This is the signal that existed between her and CuChulainn: a milking of Iuchna's spotted cows would be let loose down the river toward the men of Ulster so that the river would be white when she was washing CuRoi's head. That was done. It was let loose toward them so that the river has been called Finnglais, White Stream, since that time.

She examined his head then in front of the hill-fort.

'Come indoors into the fort so that your head can be washed before the troops come back with their burdens.'

At that he raised his head and saw Ulster's troop coming along the glen toward him both on foot and on horse.

'What is that yonder, woman?' CuRoi said.

'Your household,' the woman said, 'with stones and oaks to make the stronghold.'

[CuRoi answered:]

'If they are oaks, they skim swiftly.
They are special, if they are stones.'

He raised his head again. He scanned their companies still more.

'What is that yonder?' he said.

25

'Herds of cows and cattle,' she said.
[CuRoi spoke:]

> 'If cattle — cattle-coloured —
> they are no herds of thin cows.
> A small man bears a blade
> on the back of each last cow.'

Suddenly he perceived it the same way [as she],
and the woman washed his head.[6] She washed his
hair — and she tied it to the posts of the bed and to
the pillars. She stole his sword from its scabbard
and she opened the hillfort. He heard nothing until
the men had filled up the house on him and until
they were at his throat. He rose up at once to
attack them, and he killed a hundred of their men
with his feet and fists.

The fool who was in the house rose against them
and killed thirty of their warriors. Of him was recited:

> He was the lord's laughing man
> but playing at battle, nobly free
> he slew thirty armed men
> then suffered death himself.

After CuRoi's scream of distress, old toothy
Senfiacail came up first. It was said of him:

> From afar strode Senfiacail.
> He killed a hundred of their host.
> Though his body's might was great
> he found his grave by CuChulainn.

Then the leader of packs, Cairpre Cuanach, came

26

upon them:

> Cairpre Cuanach came upon them.
> Mighty fight: he killed one hundred
> would have menaced Conchobor
> had the swarming sea not drowned him.

That is, when he was menacing Conchobor, he saw his stronghold blazing across the sea in the north. So he went into the sea to save the stronghold. It was a long swim, and he was drowned at it.[7]

When they heard the scream of distress, the Clan Dedad threw down each standing-stone now erect or toppled in Ireland. They came to the slaughter around the hillfort. Of this was said:

> Dedad's clan came up
> to seek their king. Their count:
> five score and three hundred
> ten hundred and two thousand.

While they were butchering each other around the hillfort, CuChulainn sheared off the man's head and set fire to the fort. Then CuRoi's poet, Ferchertne, who was with his horses in the glen, spoke:

> 'What little boy changes [shape][8]
> alongside CuRoi's hillfort?
> With Daire's son alive
> it would not burn so finely.'

Afterwards CuRoi's charioteer, FerBecrach, accepted protection from Conchobor's son Cairpre and went into his chariot. But he lashed the horses

27

near a rock so that the rock smashed both horses and people. It was said of him:

> With great beauty and swiftness
> FerBecrach — certainly so —
> carried Conchobor's son Cairpre
> under the bitter salt-sea waves.

Ferchertne came up after that.
'Are you not Ferchertne?' said Conchobor.
'I am then,' he said.
'Was CuRoi good to you?' said Conchobor.
'He was good,' he said.
'Tell us something of his worth.'
'I cannot do him justice now,' Ferchertne said. 'My mind is troubled because my king has been killed, and my own hand may kill me if no other does.'
It was then that the poet Ferchertne spoke what follows, 'The Eulogy of CuRoi':[9]

> 'It is wrong
>   for my soul
> to speak what
>   has slain me
> would that
>   a woman
> had not been
>   in the lands
> of the towering noble
>   my enemies
> brought down
>   a noble champion
> most excellent
>   man of knowledge

he could fight
           sharp swords for us
he will sleep
           a sleep of early death
I will be forgotten
           like chaff
when he is gone
           a fatal absence
you may tell
           what I possessed
from that one man
           [my mouth is]
dry for him
           dry of mead
he will sleep now
           through praises
of feasts and
           sheltering fights.

CuRoi granted me
           ten holdings
of Daire's sons
           ten slavewomen
ten golden bridles
           ten noble horses
ten bordered garments
           ten cauldrons
ten straight swords
           tusk-hilted
ten fair pairs
           of victory swords
ten prows, ten hardy
           swarms of bees
ten tens of cows
           one hundred cows

ten cowherds
        for a cattle-raid
ten bitches easily loosed
        from white-metal chains[10]
        onto herds of wild deer.

CuRoi granted me
        ten vessels
ten cups of
        precious stone
ten goblets
        ten casks.
He granted me
        ten griffin claws
ten drinking horns
        metal-tipped
        of gentle-buffalo horn.

He granted me
        ten raths
ten good
        dwellings.
He pledged me
        ten hundred pigs
ten hundred
        handsome sheep
ten belts
        ten gold helmets
ten boars
        lords of lands
ten heavy-working oxen
        for splitting
        stony Ireland.

Because I had a son
        with no silver
he granted me
        ten silvery *cumals*[11]
ten herds
        of smaller stock
        mating in their tens.

He granted me
        ten male slaves
ten work horses
        ten teams
ten yokes
        of chain with
        a bright iron lock.

He granted me
        ten bright flat dishes
ten arm rings
        ten Gaulish straps
ten fire slings
        ten great vats
for copious drinking
        ten drinking bowls
ten heavy kraters
        ten sides of bacon
ten wide sheepskin cloaks
        ten coverings
ten speckled tentcloths
        ten protective cloths
        with varied forms.

He granted me
        ten golden apples[12]

ten golden earrings
        ten golden vessels
ten smaller vessels
        with the plunder
        of Babylon's foes.

He granted me
        ten red tunics
ten white shirts
        ten crested helmets
ten fair brooches
        ten fidchell sets
with lights of flame
        ten racks
of weapon sets
        and lands that
        met my full desire.

When I was in
        the great houses
of Daire's son
        he served me
drinks of ale
        goblets of wine
with nutmeats
        and shared wealth
a prince possessed
        men covered with
death's milk, intense
        intoxicating prize
for CuRoi's victories[13]
        a king suffered
a base death
        from Ulster's men

around his Erainn
       avenging justice
is reaching
       old and young
no lasting post
       as prince of Mis
steady in strife
       and slaughter
CuRoi was
       a great son
succeeding hard Daire
       swift and powerful
grandson of Dedad
       in every way
the crown
       of his ranks
was ten
       hill-giants[14]
when a hunting party
       camped by my land
when a prince
       was slain
Conchobor swiftly
       showed his left side
CuChulainn
       fought against
ear-delighting
       fellows
an icy strength
       was born
he was killed
       by a woman
by no hound[15]
       by no arms

33

tell it in hosts
          you advanced
you contrived
          to bind a fist
you spawned sleep
          with your treachery
he was left a prince
          of phantoms
he has gone hostage
          for his kingship
he was a champion
          against enemies
it is wrong
          for my soul
to speak what
          has slain me.'[16]

'That was a king's gift-giving,' said Conchobor.

'From him it was little,' said Ferchertne. 'Whereabouts is Blathnait?'

'Here she is,' the warriors said. 'The price of rescuing her was cutting off CuRoi's head.'

Then Ferchertne crushed her against the rock on the tip of Cenn Bera[17]: he rushed at her, and grasped her in his two hands so that the ribs in her back broke, and he dragged her over the cliff. The rock smashed them both, and their grave is on the shore below the rock. Of this was recited:

The joint struggle was sad
for Blathnait and Ferchertne:
both their graves are
near strong Cenn Bera.

Despite that, the slaughter mounted up each day from Samain to the middle of the spring. The Ulstermen counted their men both going and coming. They had left behind a third to a half of their chariot-fighters.

And so it was said,

> When his wife betrayed CuRoi
> she did an evil deed.
> Though she was not unscathed
> she left the Erainn shamed.[18]

> Menn's daughter Blathnait was killed
> in the slaughter at Airgetglenn.
> A woman's great deed: betraying
> her man when she is ruled by him.

'That, then, is *The Death of CuRoi*.'

THE DEATH OF CU CHULAINN

CU CHULAINN had killed a number of formidable men over the years. Calatin Dana, his twenty-seven sons, and a nephew were killed by CuChulainn in the cattle-raid of Cuailnge; Coirpre NiaFer, king of Tara, was slain by CuChulainn in the battle of Ros na Rig, undertaken to avenge the cattle-raid of Cuailnge on Ulster's ravagers; and CuRoi was slain treacherously by CuChulainn in league with Blathnait.[1] All these men had left behind children to avenge them. Calatin Dana left his wife pregnant, Coirpre NiaFer was survived by his son Erc, and CuRoi left behind his son Lugaid.

Calatin Dana's wife bore three sons and three daughters. They were blinded in their left eyes so as to give them greater access to occult powers. The sons were set to learning druidry and potion-practice, and arts of destruction. The daughters learned hidden knowledge and witchcraft. All this was for the purpose of avenging their father.

When their craft was complete, they joined with Erc son of Coirpre and Lugaid son of CuRoi to plot CuChulainn's downfall. Calatin Dana's children told Erc and Lugaid it would be only a week's work to make the preparations — a week of years! For seven years, then, they laid their plans. Calatin's sons prepared deadly spears to use against Cu-Chulainn, and the spears were set by a poisonous man named Maine.

When all was ready, the conspirators mustered an army and entered Ulster. Again, as in *Táin Bó Cúailnge*, the Ulstermen were disabled by their accursed pangs. They told CuChulainn that he should not leave Emain Macha until they were able to accompany him to battle.

'. . . until today I have not endured the grief of women and children without protecting them.'

At that fifty queens stepped in front of him. They bared their breasts to him. (They were the first to discover baring women's breasts as a means of checking CuChulainn in Emain Macha. It happened in *The Boyhood Deeds*.)[2] Three vats of water were brought to quench his heated rage. That day he was not allowed to go into battle.

'Sons of Calatin, I see that CuChulainn is not leaving them today, despite your skill at potion-practice,' Lugaid said. 'It has been a long wait at Beoil Menbolg for the men here from Dun Cermna and Beoil Con Glais and Temair Lochra and Commar Tri nUisce where the three waters meet. Your potion-practice trick is poor. It is taking a long time for CuChulainn to come.'

'Tomorrow we will get him to come.'

They were there until the next day. Calatin's children shaped hosts about Emain Macha so all Emain seemed to smoke with fire-devastation. It seemed that Emain Macha would fall to the hosts. The weapons fell from their hooks. The evil news was brought to CuChulainn.

Then Leborcham spoke:

> 'Arise, CuChulainn
>   arise to attack
> help Muirtheimne plain
>   against Leinster's men
> Lug's well-reared
>   whelp[3]
> turn to your hero's
>   battle-feats.

CuChulainn
      arise to attack
so that palms
      are beaten
for spoiling
      Muirtheimne
great portents
      warriors to fight
Cormac has not been
      let go with you
Conchobor's huge
      household is far off
Conall is
      not near by
since Cormac has not
      burst forth for us
since he does
      not aid you
with his presence
      Lugaid close kin
to one slaughtered
      will avenge an act
array yourself
      splendid attacker
grandson of Cathbad
      arise to attack.'[4]

CuChulainn spoke:

'Cease, girl
      not I alone
enjoy Conchobor's
      province
though there is a
      troublesome enemy

39

I will not
            fight alone
it is bad advice
            for me
to suffer during
            Ulster's pangs[5]
I am no eager
            chariot-fighter
greedy
            for war today.'

Then Niab, Celtchair's daughter and Conall Cernach's wife, spoke:

'For you, CuChulainn
            that is fine
Conall's
            war-chariot
a fair thing
            to be guarded
is soon bartered
            for Ulstermen
in muddied fords
            there is slashing
and lost heads
            where you see him
for the striker
            is none other
the deed is
            none other
than the rampage
            of Amairgin's
great son.'[6]

CuChulainn said:

'Truly woman
     though I was fey
I did not
     meet my match
I guarded
     my honour
my prowess
     was not stolen
I do not
     avoid my death.'

After that CuChulainn leapt to his weapons and whirled his cloak about him. The first cloak he wrapped about him tore, and his brooch fell from his hand. Then CuChulainn spoke:

'No enemy is a cloak
     which brings warning
a brooch is enemy
     which tears skin
and falls
     through a foot
spoils will be shattered
     before a shield
a blade will break
     before my right fist
I will soon shed
     proud blood
I will wound
     the choicest men
south of Muirtheimne
     great wailing
will be met
     with contempt.'[7]

41

After that he wrapped his cloak about him and took up his shield with the notched edge. Then he said to Loeg mac Riangabra, 'Friend Loeg, yoke the chariot for us.'

Now, the Morrigan had smashed the chariot the previous night. She did not want CuChulainn to go to the battle because she knew he would not return to Emain Macha.[8]

Loeg said, 'I swear by my people's god, even if Conchobor's province surrounded Liath Macha, they could not drag him to the chariot. He has not opposed you until today. The spirit that always delighted me has not appeared today. If you wish, go call the gray yourself.'

CuChulainn went to him, and three times the horse turned his left side toward CuChulainn. Then CuChulainn spoke to Liath Macha:

'Never, Liath,
        you beauty
have you
        turned to me
your left side
        in savage anger
so I will not
        act against you
I will forgive
        death's due
my intent did not falter
        on a great plain
when I drove you about
        though reins were red
horses and hosts
        were kept off.

42

```
Smashing chariot-frame
            and yoke and pads
    where we sat
            a pleasant seat
    Badb struck us
            in Emain Macha
    never.'⁹
```

At that Liath Macha came to CuChulainn and let great round tears of blood fall on his feet. CuChulainn leapt into the chariot and made a dash to the south along the Midluachair road. He saw a girl before him. She was Learning-and-Warning's own child, Leborcham, the daughter of Ai and Adarc, two slaves in Conchobor's house. Then Leborcham spoke:

```
            'Do not leave us
    do not leave us
            CuChulainn
    your face
            is worthy
    your glowing cheek
            is generous
    your finely scarred face
            is a fair face
    your destined destruction
            is a sorrow
    we will grieve for
            woe to our women!
    woe to our children!
            woe to our hopes!
    long downcast
            keening for you
    you will proceed
```

                    on a kingly course
          to the battle
                    where great ones
          will die
                    great wailing
          for Muirtheimne plain
                    when you are gone.'[10]

She said this in a loud voice. So said the three
fifties of women who were in Emain Macha.
   'It would be better not to leave them,' said Loeg,
'for you have never flouted the command of your
mother's line until today.'
   'No, alas,' said CuChulainn.

          'Take leave, Loeg
                    a charioteer tends things
          a chariot-fighter defends
                    a supporter advises
          men do manly deeds
                    and women weep
          go to the battle
                    do not accept pity
          that does not help you.'

   The chariot was turned to the left. At that the
band of women made a clamour of weeping and
wailing and beating of hands. They knew Cu-
Chulainn would not return to Emain Macha.[11]

CU CHULAINN'S LIVING PROPHETIC-
WORDS ON THE DAY HE FOUND DEATH

[CuChulainn spoke:]

'THE woman-bands
are sorrowful
            with hosts of tears
for our deaths
            by great ones
blind grief
            has found a gain
let churns
            clear away
so you can step
            from a stronghold.

With tidings
            you will have woe
princes will go off
            a man, safety's source
a famous calf
            noble red reins[12]
half-blind evil hags
            will come to crush me.

All Ulster
            will lament me
they will bury victory
            generosity will die
with enforcement
            of guarantees
the province
            will be split
by right hands.

A chariot-fighter
        in a single chariot
will drive
        a daring drive
zealous for the tribe
        he will force fights
three violent outbursts.

Eyes do not cry for things
        they do not see
great poignant grief
        the hero's breast
will wither
        because of losses
fair fight
        will be broken
a single man
        in unequal odds[13]
will attack
        between two wheels
he will have
        just vengeance.

Woe for jealousy
        in the *síd*
Liath Macha's path
        will reach
red wonders
        green youth trampled
it will be no
        gentle new custom
I will beseech
        a spirited horse
he will answer
        with forays.

I will oppose
        a hostile inroad
afterwards
        shame, shame
destruction that day
        of warriors
in my homeland
        Muirtheimne plain
I will drink a river
        streaming, swollen
my belly whole
        despite small spells
gore after feasting
        will wash over me
a deadly
        flashing fight
fragrant film of
        blood on my body
battered bodies
        slayings, spoils
the sound shakes
        one-third the earth
skilled ones
        will dispatch
heirs' small
        magic powers
a fetter brought
        to times when
a lord's lean cows
        are destroyed

I will turn back
        troops myself
when I perform
        untold feats.

47

Cry to the world
          destruction!
a grudging child
          will be born
his clientship
          will be unfree
his epoch
          will be dark
he will dupe
          a multitude
he will warp
          many people
he will know how
          to spurn rebuke
he will rule spears
          he will destroy truth
battles will be fought
          capturing leaders
cutting off limbs
          breaking bones
slicing skin
          gouging eyes
pride's false laws
          gold on rims
silver on shafts
          gems from stones
greed will flood forth
          for mountains
of lasting crystal.

Multiply good works
          for we know of
Judgment Day
          at the end of time

48

when the world
      will drown
when a Man
      among you
will be glorified
      ransoming Creation
if only you
      adore the Son
and His law
      it will be
seven times better
      for you
than for me with my
      overweening pride[14]
which I would
      put away
it would be better
      for me to do so
it would happen
      were it His will.'

At that the band of women made a clamour of
weeping and wailing, for they knew CuChulainn
would not return to Emain Macha.

The house of the foster-mother who had raised
CuChulainn was before him on the road. He would
visit it whenever he drove past it southward and
northward. She always had a vessel of drink ready
for him. He drank the drink, said farewell to his
foster-mother, and set off. He went off along the
Midluachair road across the Plain of Mugain.

He saw a wonder: before him on the road were
three hags of sorcery, blind in their left eyes. They
had cooked a lapdog on rowan stakes, with charms
and potions. It was *geis* to CuChulainn to refuse to

49

visit a hearth and eat there. It was also *geis* to him
to eat the flesh of the animal he was named for.[16]
He sped up to go past them. He knew they were
not there for his good.

One of the hags said to him, 'Come visit us, Cu-
Chulainn.'

'I will not,' CuChulainn said.

'Because the food is a dog,' she said. 'If a great
hearth were here, you would visit it. Because it is a
small one, you don't. One who cannot accept or
endure little things is not capable of great things.'

He visited them then, and the hag served him
half the dog from her left hand. CuChulainn
accepted it from her hand and put it under his left
thigh. The hand he took it with and the thigh he
put it under were seized from end to end so that
their original strength was lost.

Then they set off southward along the Midluachair road around Sliab Fuait. CuChulainn said
to Loeg, 'What can you see for us, friend Loeg?'

Loeg answered, 'Many fey men and great
spoils.'[17]

CuChulainn said:

> 'Woe! alas!
>> that charge suits
> a dark red horse[18]
>> a left side
> which rushes forward
>> should be concealed
> it will fall
>> before its time
> for horses fall swiftly
>> in harmful herbs
> alas! that we should fear

                    a pampered band
          of Ireland's men!'[19]

   As CuChulainn went southward along the Midluachair road, he could see the camp on Muirtheimne plain. He was also seen, and then it was
Erc mac Coirpri spoke:

                    'I see here
                              a fair flawless chariot
                    with well-built frame
                              with a greenish awning
                    with a great seat
                              for cunning feats
                    in the fine chariot
                              are weapons
                    of a fair-helmeted
                              feat-performer
                    that chariot is
                              behind two horses
                    fine-headed
                              round and small
                    small-muzzled
                              leaping horses
                    with bulging nostrils
                              bulging eyes
                    broad-chested
                              broad-bellied
                    though they are in step
                              equally trained
                    that team is not
                              matched in colour
                    one of the horses
                              is lynx-gray
                    leaping, massive

                              51

                        bristling, thundering
arched, skittish
            the other horse
is jet-black
            white-faced
with heavy, dark
            gloomy brows
on them are
            two high gilt yokes
in that chariot
            is a man
with fair flowing
            curly hair
a fiery red weapon
            is in his hand
blazing redly
            a glossy bird
flutters over the chief
            of that chariot
his hair in tresses
            has three colours
dark hair
            near the scalp
blood-red hair
            in the centre
a golden crown
            covers the outside
his head and hair
            are finely fixed
so three circling streams
            float about his head
like threads of gold
            on beaten gold
under the hand of a
            mighty master craftsman

or like sun shining
        on buttercups
on a summery day
        in mid May
so shines
        the dullest part
of that warrior's hair.'[20]

'There coming toward us is the man you are
expecting, men of Ireland.'

THE GREAT DEFEAT ON
MUIRTHEIMNE PLAIN

A MOUND of cut sods was raised under Erc
mac Coirpri then. A wall of shields was made
around him, and three equally fine, fierce battalions
of Ireland's men were formed. Erc said, 'Men of
Ireland, prepare for that man, CuChulainn.'
He spoke these words:

'Rise up
        men of Ireland
rise to attack
        here is CuChulainn
a checker of combats
        victorious
with a red sword
        get ready!
take heed!
        cry out!

53

heads will shriek
  because of him
you will strike
  someone to be feared
the prodding
  of a poem
for protection
  piles anger on him
he is unique
  he alone is
the son of a god
  the son of a man[21]
woe to leaders!
  woe to troops!
woe to ranks!
  woe to rulers!
a prince was born
  a fair heavenly prince
more than heavenly
  easily angered
steadfast
  truly protective
bid be manlike by
  our own world's god
he was nine months
  hidden by
an ivory girl
  a bright origin
quell Macha!
  banish our stupor!
woe! hacking
  will wreak havoc
hacking will cause
  a chief to be maimed

when keen Cu comes
rise up!'[22]

'What preparations have we made? In what way can we receive his feats?' asked the men of Ireland.

'That is easy. This is my plan for you,' Erc said. 'Four of Ireland's five provinces are here. Form a single troop of yourselves. Make an unbroken barrier of shields around and above the troop, encircling the men and covering them. Put three men on each hill around the troop. Two of the strongest ones of the host should trade blows with one another. A satirist with his hazel rod should be with them, so they can make a disgracing-demand for CuChulainn's own spear.[23] (Its name is Blad ar Bladaib, Triumph of Triumphs.) They can also demand his readied spears which can be let loose on him afterward. It is prophesied of his own spear that a king will be killed by it unless they get it from him with a demand. And give out a wailing cry and a scream of distress. Then the man will not get into a heated rage or get his horses lathered with fury. Nor will he ask for single combat with you as he did on the raid for Cuailnge's cows.'[24]

It was done as Erc said.

CuChulainn came toward the troop then. He did three thunder-feats over his chariot — a thundering of three nines of men, a thundering of a hundred, and a thundering of three hundred — to clear away the hosts from Muirtheimne plain. Cu-Chulainn came to the troop and began a round of arms-play on them. He handled his spear and his shield and his sword and his feats equally well, so that

Like grains of sea-sand
          stars in heaven
dew-drops on May Day
          flakes of snow
hailstones
          leaves in a forest
buttercups in Brega
          and grassblades
under the hoofs
          of a horse-herd
on a summer's day
          was the number of
their halved heads
          their halved skulls
their split hands
          their split feet
and their hacked
          red bones
after he scattered them
          about Muirtheimne plain.[25]

That plain was gray with their brains after the law-
less raid and the arms-play CuChulainn made on
them.

Then he saw two men exchanging blows. He did
not part them.

'You lose honour by not parting these two,' the
satirist said.

With that CuChulainn leapt down toward them,
and gave each a punch in the head so their brains
came out through their ears and noses.

'You have parted them now,' the satirist said.
'Neither is harming the other.'

'They would not quiet down when asked,' Cu-
Chulainn said.

'Give me that spear, CuChulainn,' said the satirist.

'I swear by my people's oath — your need of it is not greater than my own. Ireland's men are here attacking me, and I am attacking them.'

'I will satirize you, unless you produce it,' the satirist said.

'I have never been satirized for stinginess or stinting.' With that, CuChulainn shot him the spear, butt-end first. It went through his head and killed nine men on the other side. CuChulainn went through the troop to the very edge.

Then CuRoi's son Lugaid grasped one of three spears readied by Calatin's sons.[26]

'What will fall by this spear, sons of Calatin?' Lugaid asked.

'A king will fall by that spear,' Calatin's sons said.

Lugaid cast the spear toward the chariot, and it hit Loeg mac Riangabra. It tore out his innards and spilled them onto the chariot pads. It was then Loeg uttered [a poem beginning], 'Bitingly he wounded me.'[27]

Afterward CuChulainn removed the spear from Loeg, and Loeg bade farewell. It was then CuChulainn spoke: 'I myself will be both chariot-fighter and charioteer this very day.'

When CuChulainn reached the edge of the troop, he saw two men exchanging blows before him. A satirist with his hazel-rod was with them.

'You lose honour by not parting us, CuChulainn,' said one of the two men.

At that CuChulainn leapt down toward them and cast each of them aside. He made bits of them on a rock nearby.

'Give me that spear, CuChulainn,' the satirist said.

'I swear my people's oath — your need of the spear is no greater than my own. It depends on my hand and my valour and my weapons to clear away four of Ireland's five provinces from Muirtheimne plain today.'

'I will satirize you,' the satirist said.

'Only a single demand is required from me a day, and today I have already paid what is required of my honour.'

'I will satirize Ulster on your account,' the satirist said.

'Ulster has never been satirized for my miserliness or stinting. However little of my life remains because of it, Ulster will not be satirized today.' CuChulainn gave him the spear by the butt-end so it went through his head and killed nine men behind him. CuChulainn made his way through the troop as we said before.

Erc, Coirpre's son, seized one of the three spears readied by Calatin's sons. 'What will this spear get, sons of Calatin?' Erc mac Coirpri asked.

'That is easy. A king will fall by that spear,' said Calatin's sons.

'I heard what you thought would fall by the spear Lugaid just cast.'

'And that was true,' said Calatin's sons. 'The king of Ireland's charioteers fell by it — Cu-Chulainn's charioteer, Loeg mac Riangabra.'

'I swear my people's oath, I am not going to kill a king like the one he struck.' Then Erc let loose the spear at CuChulainn, and it hit Liath Macha.

CuChulainn snatched the spear away, and each said farewell to the other. Liath Macha left with half the yoke about his neck. He went to Linn Leith, the Gray's Pool, in Sliab Fuait. Out of it he had come to CuChulainn, and to it he went after he was wounded.[28] At that CuChulainn spoke: 'Your horse will pull a single yoke here today.'

CuChulainn thrust one of his feet under the end of the yoke and made his way through the troop in the same way. He saw before him two men exchanging blows and a satirist with a hazel rod along with them. He parted them then, and the parting he did was no worse than his parting of the other four.

'Give me that spear, CuChulainn,' the satirist said.

'Your need of the spear is no greater than my own.'

'I will satirize you,' the satirist said.

'I have paid for my honour today. Only a single demand is required from me a day.'

'I will satirize the Ulstermen on account of you.'

'I have paid for their honour,' he said.

'I will satirize your kin,' the satirist said.

'A land I have not reached will never hear scurrilous stories about me, for little is left of my life.' CuChulainn cast him the spear butt-end first, so that it went through his head and through three more groups of nine men.

'That is a favour with fury, CuChulainn,' the satirist said.

After that CuChulainn went back through the troop to the edge. Then Lugaid seized the third spear readied by Calatin's sons.

'What will this spear get, sons of Calatin?'

'A king will fall by it,' Calatin's sons said.

'I heard what you thought would fall by the

59

spear Erc cast just now.'

'That was true,' they said. 'The king of Ireland's horses fell by it — Liath Macha.'

'I swear my people's oath, I am not going to kill a king like the one he struck.' Then Lugaid cast the spear toward CuChulainn. It hit him and tore out his entrails and spilled them onto the chariot pads. Then Dub Sainglenn left him, taking half the yoke. He went into Loch Dub, the dark lake in the district of Muscraige. Out of it he had come to CuChulainn, and into it he returned.[29] At that the lake seethed.

The chariot remained alone on the plain. Then CuChulainn said, 'I would like to go as far as the lake there to get a drink.'

'We agree to that, so long as you come back to us.'

'Should I not be able to come back myself, I bind you to come for me.'

CuChulainn gathered up his entrails in his arms and went off to the lake. When he reached the lake he placed his hand about his belly and held his entrails tightly in his belly. He took a drink and washed himself. Loch Lamraith, Hand-Boon Lake, in Muirtheimne plain was named for that. (Another name for it is Loch Tonnchuil.) Then he sprang away and commanded them to come for him.

CuChulainn came to a wide land west of the lake and cast his eye over it. He went toward a standing-stone on the plain. He put his belt around it so that he would not die sitting or lying down — so that he would die standing.

The men surrounded him. They did not dare go toward him. They thought he was alive. 'You lose honour,' said Erc mac Coirpri, 'by not taking that man's head as vengeance for my own father's head which was carried off by CuChulainn and buried with Eochaid NiaFer's body.' (Eochaid's head was carried from his body, and it is in Sid Nenta over the water.)

THE VICTORIOUS ONSLAUGHTS
OF LIATH MACHA

THEN Liath Macha returned to CuChulainn to guard him while his soul was in him and his warrior's light remained shining from his brow. Liath Macha made three bloody charges around him so that fifty fell by his teeth and thirty by each of his hoofs. That is the number of the host he killed. From that slaughter there is [the saying], 'No more fierce were Liath Macha's victorious onslaughts when CuChulainn was slain.'[30]

Then a raven flew onto CuChulainn's shoulder. 'That pillar did not usually hold birds,' said Erc mac Coirpri.

So then Lugaid gathered up CuChulainn's hair from behind and struck off his head. CuChulainn's sword fell from his hand and struck Lugaid's right hand to the ground. CuChulainn's right hand was cut off as vengeance. The hosts set out, and they took CuChulainn's head and his right hand with them until they reached Tara. That is the burial site of CuChulainn's head and his right hand and the whole panel of his golden shield. Cenn Faelad mac Ailella spoke of this in 'The Deaths of the Men of Ulster':[31]

In Airrbe Rofir CuChulainn fell,
a fair tower, a strong man.
A greater guard, he beat back bands
against Lugaid, against Mac Tri Con.

A manly number clearly fell.
It was no commoner's death:
four eights, four tens
four fifties of fair chiefs.

Four thirties, a strong sum
four forties, a hard deed
four twenties, a fair find
of Sualtaim's son's strewn slayings.

In his great grief he killed
thirty kings with his casts.
Almost seven score strong champions
he left in hacked bits.

His head is far from him
a firm fighter in Tara's hill.
His head is joined to
Coirpre NiaFer's trunk.

Over the water in Sid Nenta
is Eochaid's head now.
Fair king Coirpre's head
joins Eochaid's trunk in Tethba.

The hosts set off southward till they reached the
river Liffey. When they reached the river, Lugaid
said to his charioteer, 'My full belt feels heavy
around me. I want to bathe.'
He set off in a different direction from the host,

and the host continued on. Lugaid bathed.[32] He caught a fish between his two calves. He tossed it up to his charioteer, and the charioteer struck a fire to cook the fish at once.

CONALL CERNACH'S RED RAMPAGE[33]

WHEN they had put their pangs aside, the hosts of Ulster set off from Emain Macha in the north toward Sliab Fuait. Now out of the rivalry between CuChulainn and Conall Cernach had come an agreement: whichever one of them were killed first would be avenged by the other.[34] CuChulainn had said, 'If I am killed first, how fast will you avenge me?'

'I will avenge you before sunset of the day you are killed,' Conall Cernach said. 'And if I am killed first, how fast will you avenge me?'

'I do not think your blood will be cold on the ground when I avenge you,' CuChulainn said.

So, then, when Conall Cernach was coming in his chariot in front of the host, he met Liath Macha all bloodied going to Linn Leith. Conall Cernach spoke:

> 'No yoke guides him
>   to Linn Leith
> he goes off
>   with wounds
> wrecked chariot
>   under left jaws
> with bloodstains
>   of man and horse

from the right hand
            of Lugaid.
Lugaid it is
            the son of
CuRoi mac Dairi
            who has killed
my own foster-brother
            CuChulainn.'35

Then Conall Cernach and Liath Macha went off
and circled through the carnage. They saw Cu-
Chulainn by the pillar. Liath Macha went and put
his head on CuChulainn's breast.

'Liath Macha cares about that corpse,' Conall
said.

Conall went after that and kicked the barrier of
shields. 'I swear my people's oath,' he said, 'this
could be a huge man's hedge.'

'You have named the place,' a druid said. 'The
name of this place will be Airrbe Rofir, Huge-
Man's Hedge, forever.'

Conall set off after the host then. Lugaid was
bathing at that time. 'Watch the plain for us,'
Lugaid said to his charioteer, 'so that no one can
come toward us without being seen.'

The charioteer kept watch. 'There is a single
rider coming toward us here,' he said.36 He comes
with great swiftness and speed. You would think
that Ireland's raven-flocks were above him and that
snowflakes were speckling the plain before him.'

'The rider coming here is no friend,' Lugaid said.
'That is Conall Cernach on Derg Druchtach. The
birds you saw above him are clods from the horse's
hoofs, and the snowflakes you saw speckling the
plain before him are foam from the horse's lips

and bridle-bit. Watch which way he comes.'

'He is coming toward the ford,' the charioteer said, 'the way the host came.'

'Let that horse go past us,' Lugaid said. 'We do not want a fight with him.'

When Conall Cernach reached the middle of the ford, he looked about. 'There is steam from a fish yonder,' he said.

He looked about a second time. 'There is steam from a charioteer yonder,' he said.

Conall looked about a third time. 'There is steam from a king yonder,' he said. 'I had better go to see him.'[37]

He approached them. 'Welcome is the debtor's face,' Conall Cernach said. 'Then the one who is owed debts can demand them of him. I have a claim on you for killing my comrade CuChulainn. Here I am trying to collect it from you.'

'That is not right,' Lugaid said. 'Battle with me now will not add to your valour until the trophies of my victory reach the land of Munster with me.'[38]

'I would grant that, so long as we not go along the same path as equals speaking together,' Conall Cernach said.

'It will not be hard to avoid,' Lugaid said. 'I will go this way along the Gabran roadway so that I go over Smechun gap. You go that way over Gabair and over Leinster's [Sliab] Mairge till we meet in Airgetros plain.'[39]

Lugaid was the one who arrived first. The other — Conall Cernach — came afterwards and shot a javelin at him. Lugaid's foot was against the standing-stone in Airgetros plain when it hit him. Coirthe Lugdach, Lugaid's Standing-Stone, in Airgetros plain was named for that.

After his first wound Lugaid went on till he was at Fertae Lugdach, Lugaid's Mound, among Ossairge's causeways. There they came together.

'I would like to get a fair fight from you,' Lugaid said.

'In what way?' Conall Cernach asked.

'Since I have only one hand, only one hand of yours should come against me.'

'Agreed,' Conall Cernach said. Conall's hand was tied to his side with cords.

They were there three hours of the day, and neither overcame the other. When Conall Cernach did not prevail, he looked about at his mare, Derg Druchtach, the red blood-shedder. She had a dog's head, and she used to destroy men in battles and fights. The mare came toward Lugaid and took a bite from his side. She tore out his entrails and spilled them about his feet.

'Alas, Conall Cernach,' Lugaid said, 'that is not a fair fight.'

'I only made you guaranties about myself,' Conall Cernach said. 'I made no guaranties about beasts or brainless creatures.'[40]

'I know now you will not go off until you carry off my head with you, since we ourselves took CuChulainn's head. You may take my head as well as your head, and add my own kingship to your kingship, and my weapons to your weapons,' he said, 'for I prefer you to be the best warrior in Ireland.'

Then Conall Cernach struck off Lugaid's head. He set off with the head. He met up with the men of Ulster in Roiriu, in Leinster's lands. The head was placed on a stone, and it was forgotten there.

When they reached Gris, Conall inquired, 'Has

66

one of you brought the head?'

'We have not,' they all said.

Then Conall Cernach spoke, 'I swear my people's oath, that thing is half crime.' Midbine, Half-Crime, in Roiriu was named for that. They turned back for the head. They saw a wonder: the head had melted the stone and sunk through it.

CU CHULAINN'S GHOSTLY PROPHETIC-WORDS ON THE DAY OF HIS DEATH[41]

THE ULSTERMEN did not let anyone go into Emain with victory-spoils that week. CuChulainn's spirit, however, allowed itself to appear to the fifty queens whom he had shamed the day he went to battle. They saw a wonder: CuChulainn in his ghostly chariot in the air over Emain Macha.

It was then CuChulainn chanted to them and spoke after his death:

> 'Emain, great Emain
> > great in lands
> in Patrick's lifetime
> > [priests] will till
> Emain's lands
> > they will come to you
> from Europe's Alps
> > by deep boat-water
> a holy one
> > with Succet's hosts

with shining salty tears
        they will pray
to Heaven's high king
        beyond the sky
He made Zion for us
        we will go to Him
on the day
        of Final Judgment
a fair man
        will settle
east of me
        in this same plain
farewell till
        we meet again, Emain.

Youth is
        slain, Emain
shelter is
        slain, Emain
our refuge is
        uprooted, Emain
I fell in
        battle, Emain
though I was alone
        against many
for Loeg
        I crushed men
youth is
        slain, Emain.

I will attack many men
        like a murdered man[42]
I will ride about
        a very long ride

I was crushed
            too soon
have them hasten
            to keen me
a splendid fine time
            to please me
fair treasures
            on Dechtire's dog[43]
from dark earth
            will burst forth
a heroic chariot-fighter
            a noble god
I will attack
            many dead men.

When I was one
            against a number
I called upon
            Eithniu's fair son[44]
wherever
            however it was
Aife's son
            has been buried
Loeg has died
            with his incitements
there could be no
            heavier hardship
consider, Conall
            my prophetic words
save one of
            Ulster's swift ships
chariot-hosts
            charioteers
you will have
            sea-floods

from salmon-plain
            to heart-plain.'[45]

CuChulainn spoke of Christ's coming:

        'In the beginning Christ
                lifted up the lands
        unable to fail
                the present
        He will rule
                our race
        the fair King
                will watch our fate
        Lord above us
                beneath us
        Father to the world
                a bulwark about us
        the Son of Man
                in a heavenly home
        His rule will come
                it will fill each spot
        it will stop
                your guile
        Jesus will
                vanquish Hell
        in return for
                Adam's shame
        in His kingdom
                He will keep watch
        He will guard against
                envious violence
        they will
                rejoice for Him

they will ascribe
        Heaven's law to Him.

        What tidings are these?
What blessings will
        the hosts proclaim?
The King will
        heal the earth
our Sovereign will
        shine upon us
our abodes will
        lack nothing
Heaven's strength
        for walls
wholly filled
        with thrones
an array surpassing
        princely strongholds.

After battle-victory
        the King
as One, as Two, as Three
        through His powers
which you do not
        brush aside
nor approve
        nor oppose
[will send] a dark display
        for humankind
a warning before
        death strikes
the stars of Heaven
        will shake
the bright fiery sun
        will be long absent

in a wan round path
              in the east
the moon will swell
              it will acquire
mighty brightness
              for a time.

Jesus, most noble
              most humble one
by dying
              by harrowing Hell
by assigning seats
              by releasing princes
with His full
              battle-force
with His full
              heavenly power
[will rule]
              over firmament
over men
              over creatures
forever and ever.'[46]

EMER'S LOUD LAMENT[47]

L IATH MACHA went to bid farewell to Emer.
He put his head on her breast. Three times
he circled to the right around her and Dun Imrid
and Dun Delga.

[Emer spoke:]

Liath Macha!
   great pain!
great misery!
    great outrage!
great woe
   to see you!
no fair powerful
    chariot-fighter
victorious in battle
    follows you
with soothing words
   to claim you
he does not do feats
    over your left side
in Macha's borderlands.

Umendruad's sons[48]
   a fair cloud
kings of the *síd*
   arranged
a golden course
    to subdue forts
and many tribes
   a golden child
waged war
   over your head
he guarded
   against blades
if he found sorrows
   Delga stripped of cows
the kingly fighter
   hastened up with Death.

You king of horses
            over horses
above reproach-blows
            at victories
at bird-hunts
            neither rod
nor butt nor cast
            struck you
no left hand
            that held
split shields
            struck you
no right hand
            that slashed
enemies
            struck you.

His lineage
            captured me
great dread of him
            defended me
his great oath
            sustained me
my fair
            battle-victorious
first husband
            took heed of me.

After a hard
            dark battle
and singular
            slaughter
he died
            in unequal combat

on Wednesday
          on the first day
of Harvest
          hags crushed[49]
a fighter for
          Muirtheimne's land
foul faces
          of female powers
brought to oblivion
          triumphs' gem
battle-victorious
          CuChulainn
casting down
          the great one
putting to death
          my honours
my greatness
          my valour, my giving
my rank, my deeds.[50]

          Since it was
battle-victorious
          CuChulainn
whom Time snatched
          he heaped slaughter
on Leinstermen
          and Erainn
he slashed the Erainn
          Death cut them down
because the fair
          powerful
battle-victorious
          chariot-fighter
knew he could incite
          them with insults

they would recoil
            before his valour
he chose an
            improper course[51]
and then
            his shield fell
his horse
            turned from him
his brooch
            wounded him
he went off
            pierced
his strength
            overflowed
nothing stopped
            his stride
until he met
            half-blind hags
before him
            they cooked
a gray dog
            a great snare
to hold
            his flesh
in their evil
            possession
from his sole
            to his crown
the warrior
            was half-dead
after he met them.

His most splendid
            horse fell

Liath with keen
        Dub Sainglenn
to a bad grave
        to a vast host
he fell
        but he had
a single foot
        a single hand
no strength
        after his injury.[52]

CuChulainn killed eight named Lath, eight
named Niath, eight named Fiacc, eight named
Oengus, eight named Fiachu, eight named Fergus,
eight named Faelgus, nine named Doelgus, nine
named Saergus, nine named Illann, nine doomed
men, nine druids, ten named Bruide, ten named
Bran, ten named Brenann, ten named Coirpre, ten
named Crimthann, ten named Conaire, ten named
Conall, twenty kings, twenty defenders, twenty
splendid chariot-fighters, twenty ollams, forty
charioteers, forty landowners, one hundred pirates,
one hundred old men, one hundred youths, and
one hundred middle-aged men. He split forty
breasts and one hundred skulls. He struck off eight
hundred right hands, and he blinded eight hundred
left eyes. He left the whole host maimed on that
one day.[53]

Misery!
        Liath Macha
he has not come
        with two matched horses
before his chariot
        great grief!

77

he has not arrived
        with his two hands whole
misery!
            red-sworded Conchobor
did not counsel him
            grief!
horse-lipped Eirge
        did not find him
misery!
            good-speaking Sencha
did not reach him
            grief!
long-haired Fiacha
        did not sway him
misery!
            beautiful Eogan
did not speak to him
            grief!
Findchaem's son Fergna
        did not preserve him
misery!
            Lete's son Fergus
did not go to him
            grief!
red-bladed Feidlimid
        did not watch over him
misery!
            mighty-deeded Munremur
did not honour him
            grief!
famous Amairgin
        did not fear for him
misery!
            noble, kingly Rochad

did not guarantee him
          grief!
that all
          Ulster's heroes
were not
          in the place
where he fell
          to unequal odds
for his white
          wounded body
would ride
          for Ulster
against many peoples
          many hosts.

Misery!
          Conall Cernach
did not succour him
          grief!
triumphant Celtchair
          did not hear him
misery!
          victorious Loegaire
did not fight by him
          grief!
Fergus mac Rossa
          did not reach him
misery!
          that all Ulster
was not about him
          in the place
where he fell.[54]

Grief for him
          has crushed me

loss of him
            has cut me down
his death
            has made me weak
I am barren
            without him
I have
            nothing now.

Each heart
            that loved him
should break
            each ear
that heard of him
            should never forget
each tear
            that were ever wept
should be to mourn him
            everlastingly
each eye
            that saw him
should weep
            showers of blood
for the world
            will end in grief
now he is dead.

I will be seen with
            no other spouse
there will be
            no man-faces
boisterous
            and gift-giving
at my betrothal
            for I will find

no spouse equal
          to CuChulainn.

There will
          be sorrow
Delga
          stripped of cows
no women's
          victory-welcomes.
MesGegra
          of many deeds
has perished[55]
          he was able
to achieve
          great vengeance
he got away
          with treachery
he struck swiftly
          deadly deeds
in Siamrach plain.
          Conall lashed out
together with Cormac[56]
          and avenged
his foster-child
          with haste.

A great one
who could take up
          single combats
after carrying off
          a woman of the *síd*[57]
sought me
          a fine wooing
by goddess
          Dechtire's son

Sualtaim's
              vindication
Lug's special
              fosterling
with the trophy
              of a torque
from Scathach
              the seer
he drove about
              and banished
terror from
              Ulster's fords.

Say that I knew
              an enchanted time
as his spouse
              sixteen years.

We are due
              an end to pain
we follow
              the shadowy tribes
and peoples
              each of us
from augury
              to certainty
we weep
              for each other
we lament
              for each other
we have pity
              on each other
life now
              is wretched

we will not meet
        another day
Liath Macha![58]

NOTES

INTRODUCTION

1 By highlighting the actions of CuRoi and CuChulainn that contribute to their own destruction, we also show the affinities of these Irish death tales to the tradition of European epic as a whole. The heroes of the *Iliad* and the *Odyssey* are far from perfect, and the classical theme of hubris which results in a hero's ultimate undoing is also widespread in Greek tradition. That medieval heroes are similarly flawed and that their actions and choices may contribute to their deaths is seen, for example, in *The Song of Roland*.

2 Julius Pokorny, 'Germanish-Irisches', *Zeitschrift für celtische Philologie* 13 (1919), 123.

3 We hear rather little in the LL version of the slaughter CuChulainn wreaks; the focus remains on his death more than on his deeds. There are, however, elements in the LL version that relate to the motif of CuChulainn's own deeds before his death, including the poem on p.56 and the enumeration of those he killed on p.77. These elements could form the nucleus of a tale with the flavour of *Seisrech Breislige*, 'The Sixfold Slaughter', in *Táin Bó Cúailnge* (see Thomas Kinsella, trans., *The Táin* [Dublin, 1969], pp. 147-56), but as we have the LL version they are minor components.

   It is also worth noting that in the earliest manuscript of the fifteenth-century version, the tale is called *Oidedh Con Colainn*. On this point see A. G. Van Hamel, ed., *Compert Con Culainn and Other Stories* (Dublin, 1933), pp. 69-72.

4 The medieval foliation of the Book of Leinster indicates that only a single leaf has been lost at this point (W. O'Sullivan, 'Notes on the Scripts and Make-up of the Book of Leinster', *Celtica* 7 [1966], oversize page 1). My estimate of the number of lost lines presupposes that 45 lines in one column of the lost leaf were devoted to the completion of *Aided Celtchair meic Uithechair*, 'The Death of Celtchair mac Uithechair'. The length of the latter can be determined on the basis of a second manuscript of the tale,

Edinburgh lx, which follows LL closely in the first part of the story (cf. Kuno Meyer, *The Death-Tales of The Ulster Heroes* [Dublin, 1906], pp. 24-31). I have assumed that *The Death of CuChulainn* followed this text immediately in the first column of the recto of the lost leaf. If, however, the scribe began the new saga at the top of the second column of the lost leaf, leaving the remainder of the first column blank, probably slightly fewer words are lost.

5   See Rudolf Thurneysen, *Die irische Helden- und Königsage bis zum siebzehnten Jahrhundert* (Halle, 1921), p. 432.

6   Thurneysen, *Heldensage*, p. 437, dates the Laud 610 version as twelfth century. However, his dating here may not be entirely reliable since it is based primarily on a hypothetical manuscript stemma rather than on linguistic criteria. Thurneysen also argues that the YBL version of the tale is based on Laud 610 and represents an expansion of the briefer version; differences in the wording and the action, however, suggest to me that they represent independent summaries or transcriptions of similar oral tales.

7   See R. I. Best, ed. and trans., 'The Tragic Death of CúRói Mac Dári', *Eriu* 2 (1905), 18, and Thurneysen, *Heldensage*, p. 440.

8   Pokorny, p. 120.

9   Kuno Meyer, ed. and trans., 'Brinna Ferchertne', *Zeitschrift für celtische Philologie 3* (1899), 41.

10 Thurneysen makes the case for separating the quatrains beginning with the visionary formula from the rest of the stanzas of *Brinna Ferchertne* in 'Die Sage von CuRoi', *Zeitschrift für celtische Philologie 19* (1913), 202 ff. (cf. *Heldensage*, p. 437 ff.).

The Apocalypse of the New Testament is a good example of visionary or prophetic poetry in the past tense; it gives us a touchstone for evaluating this feature of *Brinna Ferchertne*. CuChulainn's prophecies in *The Death of CuChulainn* also use the past tense extensively.

THE DEATH OF CU ROI

1 The opening simulates the beginning of an oral per-
formance of the tale. The story begins when a question from the audience elicits a tale from the story-
teller. The text then moves into direct narrative, and
the story-teller's persona fades. He reappears briefly
at the end to conclude the tale. For a similar presentation of oral narration in a literary mode see Joel
Chandler Harris's *Uncle Remus, His Songs and His
Sayings.*
2 'Iuchna's three red-spotted cows': *na teora herca
Iuchna.* The word *erc* denotes a cow of some specific
type. The original meaning of the word is 'speckled,
dark-red, bloody, blood-red'. By extension it was used
to refer to animals with this colouring: fish, especially
trout or salmon; cows; and some type of lizard (*A
Dictionary of the Irish Language* [Dublin, Royal Irish
Academy, in progress, 1913-   ], 'E', col. 164;
hereafter cited as *DIL*). The Welsh cognate *erch* also
refers primarily to dappled colouring (*Geriadur Pri-
fysgol Cymru, A Dictionary of the Welsh Language,*
vol. 1 [Cardiff, Univ. of Wales Press, 1950-67], p. 1229,
col. 2). Speckling or dappling can be a sign of magical
or supernatural qualities in early Irish literature. Thus,
otherworldly figures at times wear speckled or dappled
clothes, and salmon — the speckled fish that could
also be called *erca* — are associated with supernatural
knowledge (e.g., T. P. Cross and C. H. Slover, eds.,
Ancient Irish Tales [1936; rept. ed., New York, 1969],
pp. 365, 505-7, hereafter cited as *Ancient Irish Tales*;
Whitley Stokes, ed. and trans., 'The Prose Tales in the
Rennes Dindsenchas', *Revue celtique* 15 [1894],
456-57).
   A second possible interpreation of *erc* is 'white
red-eared cow' (*DIL*, 'E', col. 164). While such a breed
of cow was common in Celtic areas until modern times,
white red-eared animals have special significance in
the literature, particularly in Welsh literature. In the
Welsh laws we find that the violation of the honour of
the lord of Dinefwr is to be compensated by 'as many
white cattle with red ears as shall extend one after the

other between Argoel and the Court of Dinefwr, with a bull of the same colour as them with each score of them' (Melville Richards, trans., *The Laws of Hywel Dda, The Book of Blegywryd,* [Liverpool, 1954], p. 25). Similarly, violation of the honour of the king of Aberffraw is compensated by 'one hundred cows for each cantref which may be his, and a white red-eared bull along with each hundred cows' (translated from Aled Rhys William, ed., *Llyfr Iowerth, A Critical Text of the Venedotian Code of Medieval Welsh Law* [Cardiff, 1960], p. 2). At the very least we can conclude from these references that white red-eared cattle were known for their excellence, and were considered fit for royalty. More to the point, perhaps, is the reference in *Pwyll,* the first branch of the *Mabinogi,* where white red-eared dogs belong to Arawn, king of Annwn, the otherworld (Gwyn Jones and Thomas Jones, trans., *The Mabinogion* [London, 1949], p. 3).

Thus, whatever meaning we adopt for *erca,* we are led to conclude that the *erca Iuchna* are at the very least remarkable cows and probably supernatural ones.

Magical cows also appear in modern Irish folklore where widespread stories tell of a cow which has an inexhaustible milk supply or which can fill any vessel; she often disappears when she is milked into a sieve. In many accounts the cow is owned by a giant smith from whom she is stolen by the fearsome Balor. Modern tradition usually calls the magic cow 'Glas Ghaibhleann (Ghaibhneach, Gowna)', the first element of which means 'grey' (Seán O Súilleabháin, *A Handbook of Irish Folklore* [1942; rept. ed., Detroit, 1970], pp. 483, 497; for an example of one of these stories see Seán O Súilleabháin, *The Folklore of Ireland* [London, 1974], pp. 18-22). The various affinities between the story of the magical cows of modern tradition and the story of the *erca Iuchna* — including their milk-producing capacities, the motif of robbery by a fearsome hero, and possibly even the notion that their milk is wasted (by being dumped into a river in *The Death of CuRoi*) — reinforce the supernatural interpretation of the nature of these cows suggested by the term *erc.*

I am indebted to John Bollard for his thoughts on

this subject and for his help with the Welsh references in this note.

3 This story is found in *Ancient Irish Tales*, pp. 347-54, esp. pp. 352-53.

4 This episode is extremely distilled. CuChulainn avoids Ulster because he can't avenge his shame. Thus, the action is at a standstill, and fate is suspended. Cu-Chulainn discovers the identity and whereabouts of his unknown assailant by following a flock of black birds. The birds, thus, have a fatal and supernatural dimension: they advance the fates of the principal characters, and they cause death and war.

The motifs of following birds and birds' revealing information are found elsewhere in early Irish literature. They are prominent, for example, in *Compert Con Culainn*, 'The Birth of CuChulainn' (*Ancient Irish Tales*, pp. 134-35), and *Togail Bruidne DaDerga*, 'The Destruction of DaDerga's Hostel' (Ibid., pp. 96-97).

It is appropriate for this deadly flock to be black birds. The war-goddesses Badb, Nemain, and the Morrigan often appear as ravens; and Badb means 'raven' or 'crow'. These female figures are primarily concerned with war and death and bloodshed, and frequently appear at battles. But also, like the birds that CuChulainn follows, they are involved with fate. The Morrigan appears as the washer at the ford in *Cath Maige Tuired*, 'The Second Battle of Mag Tuired' (Ibid., p. 38), determining who will die in the battle. She also claims to foresee CuChulainn's fate and to control it in *Táin Bó Regamna*, 'The Cattle-raid of Regamna' (Ibid., p. 213). See, too, her role in *The Death of CuChulainn*, p. 42.

Still another aspect of the episode is CuChulainn as a guardian of Ulster's borders. We see him guarding the borders in many tales including *Táin Bó Cúailnge* itself (Kinsella, *The Táin*, passim). In some tales he is shown watching Ulster's border with the sea and warding off invaders from the sea. He does this in *Aided Guill meic Carbada ocus Aided Gairb Glinne Rige*, 'The Death of Goll and Garb'; *Comrac ConCulainn re Senbecc*, 'The Combat of CuChulainn with Senbecc'; and *Aithed Emere le Tuir nGlesta*, 'The Elopement

89

of Emer with Tuir Glesta'. In the Derbforgaill episode of *Tochmarc Emire*, 'The Wooing of Emer' (*Ancient Irish Tales*, pp. 169-70), as here, he opposes the entry of sea birds into Ulster; there too the birds have supernatural qualities, though rather different ones from those of the birds in this story. Finally, in *Echtra Nerai*, 'The Adventures of Nera', it is said, 'It was one of [CuChulainn's] taboos that birds should feed on his land, unless they left something with him' (Ibid., p. 252). Thus, as guardian of the borders, CuChulainn is obliged to oppose the flock of black birds when they fly towards him over the sea and to follow them when they invade Ulster.

5. This is apparently an etymological gloss assimilated into the narrative. *Fir Falga*, 'the men of Falga', are equated at times with the Manx (Edmund Hogan, *Onomasticon Goedelicum* [Dublin, 1910], p. 423).

Blathnait's identity varies from text to text. In the YBL version of *The Death of CuRoi* she is called both daughter of Menn (pp. 23, 35) and daughter of Iuchna p. 25). In the versions of the tale in Laud 610 and Egerton 88 she is called 'daughter of Menn or of Puill (Poll?) mac Fidaig' (see Kuno Meyer, 'Addenda to M. de Jubainville's *Catalogue de la littérature épique de l'Irlande', Revue celtique* 6 [1884], 187 and Best, 'Death of CúRói', p. 34).

In the Egerton 88 version she is also called 'daughter of Midir'; and the same patronymic is found in the *dindshenchas* article on Findglais in the Book of Lecan (Ibid., p. 21 note a and p. 34). Finally a variant in the Egerton 88 version names her 'Bláithine the daughter of Conchobor' (see Thurneysen, 'Die Sage von CuRoi', p. 190 ff.).

6 Best, 'Death of CúRói', p. 25) translates 'thereupon he goes inside'. I am construing *inund* adverbially 'in the same way, identically' (reading *inunn* rather than *innonn* 'yonder', to that side).

7 The manuscript includes a quatrain at this point with no prose introduction:

> The fight of Daire's son Eochaid
> from the headland to the glen
> was worthy: he killed a hundred
> avenging his good king.

90

It may represent a later accretion from *Ferchertne's Dream-Vision.*

8 This may be a reference to CuChulainn's *ríastrad*, his 'warp-spasm'. Cf. Kinsella, *The Táin*, pp. 150-51.

9 In the translation of *The Eulogy of CuRoi* I have followed the order of H.3.18 as it is edited by Whitley Stokes in 'The Eulogy of CúRói, Amra Chonrói', *Eriu* 2 (1905), 1-14. Readings from both other manuscripts, YBL and Egerton 88, were collated in order to establish a good basis for translation. All deviations from the readings of H are noted, but the notes do not indicate the variant readings of the other two manuscripts. See Stokes's critical apparatus for a more complete account of the other two manuscripts.

The mixture of poetry and prose in this tale is superficially like the composition of most Ulster texts. Unlike most texts, however, all the poetry of the YBL *Death of CuRoi* has variants elsewhere. The quatrains on p. 23 are similar to stanzas in *Siaburcharpat Con-Culainn*, 'The Phantom Chariot of CuChulainn' (see note 3, above). Lines similar to those on pp. 25-26 are found in *Mesca Ulad*, 'The Intoxication of the Ulstermen', and the Laud 610 version of *The Death of CuRoi* (*Ancient Irish Tales*, pp. 224-25; Meyer, 'Addenda', p. 188). The quatrains on pp. 26-28, 34-35 are from *Ferchertne's Dream-Vision* with the exception of the quatrain beginning 'What little boy changes [shape]'. The latter is found in the Laud 610 version of the saga (see Meyer, 'Brinna Ferchertne', passim, and Meyer, 'Addenda', p. 188). Finally, as noted in the introduction, *The Eulogy of CuRoi* is found independently in H.3.18 and, thus, may represent an independent composition.

The presence of the same verse in more than one text may simply indicate that the compiler made a literary pastiche of everything he could find pertaining to CuRoi. But it may also indicate that the verse in Old Irish tales was memorized by oral tellers and formed an essential element of their repertory for recreating prose narratives. The latter case is parallel to the nature of runs in modern Irish folktales (cf. James H. Delargy, 'The Gaelic Story-Teller', *Proceed-*

ings of the British Academy 31 [1945], 209). In that case (as perhaps in this text) a story-teller could have brought together memorized verse in non-traditional ways.

With the exception of *The Eulogy of CuRoi* which requires more extensive treatment, the differences that exist between the verses in the YBL text of *The Death of CuRoi* and the other texts in which the same verses are found suggest to me variants more characteristic of oral transmission than textual transmission.

10   'White-metal chains', literally 'chains of *findruine*', an amalgam ranked in value below gold and above bronze. After *findruine* H adds 'or silver'.

11   Literally, 'ten white *cumals*'. A *cumal* is a unit of value, generally equivalent to three milch cows. Here the *cumals* are given in white metal, probably silver but possibly *findruine*.

12   'Apples', *ubla*, might also be translated 'balls'. Perhaps they are bobs for fastening or decorating tresses and braids of hair. In *Serglige ConCulainn*, 'The Sick-Bed of CuChulainn', Labraid Luathlam-ar-claideb is described as having 'yellow hair of beautiful colour, with a golden apple [*ubull*] fastening it' (Myles Dillon, ed., *Serglige Con Culainn* [Dublin, 1953], ll. 472-73); similarly in *The Destruction of DaDerga's Hostel* the description of Etain tells that 'on her head were two golden-yellow tresses, in each of which was a plait of four strands, with a bead [*mell*] of gold at the point of each strand' (*Ancient Irish Tales*, p. 94). A pair of such ornamental lock-fasteners for the hair, dating from the late Bronze Age in Ireland, is preserved in the National Museum of Ireland (cf. *Treasures of Early Irish Art, 1500 B.C. to 1500 A.D.*, ed. G. Frank Mitchell et al. [New York, 1977], no. 11).

Apparently balls of gold were also used to decorate clothing, particularly cloaks. In *Culhwch and Olwen*, Culhwch is described as wearing 'a four-cornered mantle of purple upon him, and an apple [*aual*] of red gold in each of its corners; a hundred kine was the worth of each apple' (Jones and Jones, *The Mabinogion*, p. 97).

13   Warriors were rewarded for their service to their over-

lord with drink, especially mead, wine, and ale; and in the Ulster Cycle the availability of drink in Conchobor's household is often emphasized. In early Welsh tradition there are also many examples of drink being used to bind lords to their dependents, and of fighters determined to 'earn their mead'. *The Gododdin* gives us an example of a North British ruler, Mynyddog, who gathered a picked warband and fed them for a year on mead before sending them out to fight. The warriors were slaughtered, and their eulogies refer over and over to the earlier feast of mead, wine, and malt. In one verse the poet comments, 'the pale mead was their feast and it was their poison' (Kenneth Hurlstone Jackson, trans., *The Gododdin, The Oldest Scottish Poem* [Edinburgh, 1969], p. 118).

There is a similar figure here: the intoxicating drink that CuRoi's warriors end up drinking is death's milk, a poisonous drink of death.

14 *Reraig brega*, literally 'aged men of a hill'. The word *reraig* occurs in the glosses where it is explained as those 'who were before the Flood' (*Contributions to A Dictionary of the Irish Language* [Dublin, Royal Irish Academy, in progress, 1942-   ], '*R*', col. 48).

The sense here is not completely clear. Antediluvian animals and people were thought to be of huge stature, and this may be a reference to such men (Ibid., '*D*', cols. 107-8). Alternately it may suggest that CuRoi had supporters from the other world. For modern folk beliefs dealing with supernatural inhabitants of hills see Máire MacNeill, *The Festival of Lughnasa* (London, 1962), passim.

15 This is an allusion to CuChulainn, indicating that he deserves no credit for CuRoi's death.

16 *Textual notes* to *The Eulogy of CuRoi.* S. I: after 'slain me' H adds an obscure synonym for the verb; 'most excellent man of knowledge', or 'a man of knowledge who bestowed (gifts)', reading *ro-maith*; 'when he is gone, a fatal absence', reading *iar n-err ecnairc n-airc*; for 'dry for him, dry of mead' H reads literally 'dry of mead, dry for that one man'. S. 3: 'ten casks', H adds 'or small mugs', in the original this line ends a stanza. S. 4: 'ten good dwellings', in the original this

line is longer by two (obscure) words and it ends a stanza; 'ten gold helmets', the reading 'gold' is supplied from YBL; 'ten boars, lords of lands', after this line H adds 'ten slavewomen', a gift already mentioned in s. 2; 'for splitting stony Ireland', the reading of YBL, H reads 'great or stony Ireland'. S. 5: 'of smaller stock', H adds 'or small herds'. S. 7: 'drinking bowls', *olcha* (Egerton 88 *olchua*), might be read 'ten dwellings' (cf. *Contributions*, 'C', col. 10); 'ten wide sheepskin cloaks, ten coverings', I have inverted the order of the clauses in the original, 'ten coverings' follows Pokorny's translation of *ru* as 'decke' ('Germanisch-Irisches', p. 119); 'with varied forms' is followed by several partially legible words (Stokes, 'Eulogy', p. 4). S. 8: after 'of Babylon's foes' H adds *.x. talliama taraeda iluamand* which is partially redundant with a gift mentioned in s. 7 'ten fire (?) slings'; the meaning of *iluamand* is obscure. S. 9: three lines are omitted at the end of this stanza; they seem to derive from a fragment measuring CuRoi's gifts in thirties rather than in tens:

> thirty bridles
> > thirty horses
> thirty wheels
> > granted with
> > > a splendid horse team.

S. 10: 'shared wealth' follows the reading of Egerton 88, H reads 'a chief with wealth' (reading *conn co tlus*) and YBL reads 'with intensity' (reading *co ndlus*); 'around his Erainn', literally 'because it is about (concerning) . . .'; 'avenging justice', *de-ruich* is either the perfect of *do-fich* ('justice which has avenged'), or the present with *ro* of possibility ('justice which can avenge'); after 'the crown' H adds 'or sword'; 'Conchobor swiftly showed', expanding the noun as nom. sg.; 'you advanced' follows the reading of YBL; 'it is wrong for my soul / to speak what has slain me' is omitted in H and supplied here from YBL.

Note that many of the additional words in H are petrified glosses.

17 The placename Cenn Bera might have been interpreted as 'Judge's Head' with the notion that the

rock itself passed the sentence of doom on Blathnait
(cf. *Contributions, 'B'*, col. 81).

18 This quatrain is found only in Egerton 88.

THE DEATH OF CU CHULAINN

1 The account of the death of Calatin Dana (there called
Gaile Dána) is found in Kinsella, *The Táin*, pp. 166-67;
the death of Coirpre NiaFer is told in Edmund Hogan,
ed. and trans., *Cath Ruis na Ríg for Bóinn* (Dublin,
1892), pp. 50-53.

2 This story is found in Kinsella, *The Táin*, p.76 ff.

3 The story of CuChulainn's birth is found in Ibid.,
p. 21 ff. CuChulainn's mother is Dechtire; his father is
Lug, a Celtic god; and his mortal father is Sualtaim.

4 *Textual notes*: 'Cormac has not been let go with you',
emending *cotalgad* to a form of *do-léici* 'lets loose';
'an act', specifically by extension, 'a deed of prowess,
a slaying'.

5 Literally, 'it is bad advice, my fatigue along with (or
'after') their fatigue'. The pangs of Ulster strike when
Ulster is most pressed; they are a result of a curse
on the Ulstermen. CuChulainn is exempt from the
pangs because his father is not an Ulsterman. For the
story of the origin of the pangs see Ibid., p. 6 ff. and
68 ff.

6 *Textual notes*: 'war-chariot', reading *níthcharpat* or
nétcharpat; 'there is slashing', reading *bíth* as the
verbal noun of *benaid* 'strikes'. 'Lost heads' is literally 'loaned heads'. *Oin* is a loan without interest or
without charge if it is not returned within a specified
time. There may also be a pun intended on *úan*,
'lamb': 'lambs' heads'. 'None other', *na aill*, cf. *Contributions, 'A'*, col. 117.

7 *Textual note*: 'I will wound the choicest men', reading
crechtnaigfit as I sg. future of *crechtnaigid* 'wounds'
with a suffixed pronoun.

8 The translation departs here from the order of the
manuscript. These two sentences are found in the
original after the sentence 'three times the horse
turned his left side toward CuChulainn' (p. 42). The

Morrigan is a war goddess who seems here to have knowledge, if not control, of fate (cf. note 4, *The Death of CuRoi*).

9 *Textual notes*: 'I will forgive', reading *donothlogmar* as a deponent form of *do-luigi* 'forgives'; 'my intent did not falter', a conjecture, the verb *thintla* is obscure.

10 *Textual notes*: 'woe to our hopes!' can also be 'woe to our eyes!'; 'where great ones will die', reading *ara-mbebat aird*. The wording of this poem in the original is extremely suggestive of double entendres. One might almost translate

    the chance of your
        destroying is fair
    there is gloom for which
        we will grieve . . .
    it is long
        for lament of gloom
    you will proceed on
        a kingly course
    where great ones
        will die
    on a great day
        for Muirtheimne plain
    after your course.

Aside from the opening lines 'do not leave us / do not leave us' which are unambiguous, the poem is full of word play. Are we to imagine that Leborcham says one thing and CuChulainn hears another?

11 Turning to the left here is unlucky. This is the evil omen that makes the women lament with fear and certainty that CuChulainn will not return safely.

12 The poem is alluding to CuChulainn, Loeg, and Liath Macha. Loeg's name means 'calf'.

13 For 'a single man in unequal odds / will attack' (reading *for-géba*) we might translate 'spear feats in single combat, many unequal odds' (cf. *DIL, 'F',* col. 336). This second reading suggests a version of the saga which included a series of single combats much like those of *Táin Bó Cúailnge*.

14 The reference here to 'overweening pride' relates to the question of the heroes' faults discussed in the Introduction (cf above, pp. 12-14, note 1 to the Introduction, and below, note 51).

15   *Textual notes* to 'CuChulainn's Living Prophetic-
Words'. S. 1: 'for our deaths by great ones', possibly
to be read 'to shelter us from great ones' (or 'from
plains'); 'let churns clear away', reading the verb as a
form of *fo-scuichi* 'moves away'. S. 3: 'with enforcement of guarantees', reading *baçc* as 'hindrance', but
possibly should be read 'from corners of raths'. S. 5:
'will wither because of losses', the verb can also be
translated 'will diminish, become obsolete', and 'losses'
might also be translated 'absences'; thus, this line can
be interpreted on two levels, either indicating that his
honour demands he go forth to check the damage,
or indicating he will be destroyed because he goes
alone. S. 6: I have reversed the order of the first two
lines; 'he will answer', literally 'he will repay (a debt)'.
S. 7: 'battered bodies', the modifier is obscure so the
reading is conjecture, 'bodies' is literally 'frames' (of
bodies or chariots); 'blood on my body', or 'wounds
on my body'; 'myself / when I perform untold feats',
the text is difficult here, perhaps should be read
canisin 'ourselves' with the verb as a form of *beirid*
compounded with the intensive *immar-* (?). S. 8: I
have reversed the order of the first two lines; 'cap-
turing leaders . . . gouging eyes', aside from 'bones',
the nouns are singular, giving an effect similar to the
English 'cutting the limb, slicing the skin, gouging the
eye'; 'gold on rims / silver on shafts', cf. *urra* 'rim'
(Patrick S. Dineen, *An Irish-English Dictionary* [1927;
rept. ed., Dublin, 1965, p. 1303), but perhaps *aurrae*
'leader, chief' is the better word, giving a translation
'gold on leaders'; 'greed will flood forth for mountains / of lasting crystal', there are agreement problems here and the line seems to need emendation.
S. 9: 'we know of / Judgment Day at the end of time /
when . . .', literally 'we know upon Him at the end of
His Judgment a day when . . .'.

16   The statement of the first prohibition is literally 'it
was *geis* to CuChulainn not to visit a hearth and eat
there'. His decision to speed up when he sees the hags
indicates, however, that CuChulainn is not obliged to
visit every hearth he passes, only those to which he is
invited. The second prohibition is based on his name

97

which means 'Culann's dog or 'the hound of Culann'. The explanation of how he acquired this name is found in Kinsella, *The Táin*, p. 82 ff.

17 Loeg delivers a good portent. The usual sense of *coscar* 'spoils' is 'victory, triumph' or 'slaughter'. Here it is used in a concrete sense (*Contributions*, 'C', col. 491).

18 This may be a reference to Conall Cernach's horse which is named Derg Druchtach, 'the red blood-shedder'.

19 *Textual notes*: there are problems with the case of 'a dark red horse', perhaps should be read *eoch dubderg*; 'it will fall before its time', reading *a rae* 'its time' where Stokes reads *arae*, 'charioteer', and translates 'first the charioteer will fall / soon after the horses will fall . . .' (my translation from the French text in *L'Epopée celtique en Irlande*, ed. Henri d'Arbois de Jubainville [Paris, 1892], p. 337); 'we should fear', literally 'that we have feared'; 'a pampered band' from *meschuire*, 'a band of household retainers', which is a compound of *mes*, 'fosterling'.

20 *Textual notes*: 'small-muzzled' might be emended to modify *crú* 'hoofs' (omitted from the translation here) so as to read 'with small tapering hoofs'; after 'arched, skittish' there is an obscure word; 'a fiery red weapon', possibly a lance; 'a glossy bird', *enblaith*, literally 'a smooth bird', is glossed *longaile* 'black bird of battle'; 'like threads of gold on beaten gold', literally 'like threads of gold thread across gold from an anvil', perhaps referring to gold filigree on a gold surface; 'the dullest part', literally 'the remotest part'.

21 See above, note 3.

22 *Textual notes*: 'woe to leaders . . . rulers', probably all should be read as singular, e.g. 'woe to the leader' (reading *mind-duine*); 'truly protective', reading *fírclith*; 'bid be manlike by', literally 'manlike on account of' (*ra* for *fri* here as elsewhere in *LL*); 'our own world's god', *art* 'god' is a term used of pagan deities; 'an ivory girl, a bright origin', literally 'a girl, ivory-bright of origin'; 'quell Macha', reading *machid*; 'keen Cu', reading *aicher*.

23 The original here is plural, 'spears'. This paragraph suggests a version of the saga in which CuChulainn is

killed by his own weapons, whereas later in the narrative and in sentences from the lost opening preserved in H.3.18, we have indications that the fatal weapons were carefully prepared by Calatin's offspring. The sentence naming CuChulainn's (single) spear may represent an old gloss which has been absorbed into the text. Cf. note 26, below.

24 The single combats form the central section of *Táin Bó Cúailnge*; see Kinsella, *The Táin*, p. 114 ff.

25 The starting run of lyrical similes for dismembered bodies is apparently a traditional figure for heroic slaughter. Echoes of the same run are found, for example, in *The Second Battle of Mag Tuired* and *The Destruction of DaDerga's Hostel*. It was apparently used frequently enough to be parodied in *Aislinge Meic Conglinne*, 'The Vision of MacConglinne'. See *Ancient Irish Tales*, pp. 41, 46, 115, 118, 554.

26 The narrative has some loose ends here. The teller refers to three spears prepared by Calatin's sons for the express purpose of bringing down CuChulainn, Loeg, and Liath Macha. It is prophesied of each of these weapons that it will kill a king. This is also true of CuChulainn's own spear (see p. 55). The manuscript seems to mix elements from two ways of telling the story of CuChulainn's death — one version in which he is assailed by specifically prepared weapons and another version in which CuChulainn's spear is turned against him after being successfully elicited from him three times by threats from satirists. Both of these possibilities are common heroic patterns. The conflation of the two patterns results in CuChulainn's spears being taken from him but not used by the opponents and in the prophecy about his weapon going unfulfilled. The teller has rationalized the situation by suggesting that 'a king will be killed by [CuChulainn's spear] *unless* they get it from him with a demand'. Cf. note 23 above.

27 The manuscript has 'Bitingly he wounded me, etc.'. Often scribes included only the first line of a (possibly once well-known) poem rather than copying the entire text. The omission conserved labour and vellum, and was indicated by 'etc.' or 'et reliqua'. This is apparently

99

a case in point. Here, as in other sagas, the complete text of the poem has been lost because it was nowhere preserved in its entirety.

28 The story of how CuChulainn obtained Liath Macha and Dub Sainglenn is told in *Fled Bricrend, The Feast of Bricriu,* ed. and trans. George Henderson (London, 1899), pp. 38-39.

29 See above, n. 28.

30 Literally 'so it is from that there is . . .'. Following Stokes, I am reading *nit áithiu.*

31 Cenn Faelad mac Ailella was a famous poet and native historian. He composed a synchronism of the Irish kings and the Roman emperors, and he is credited with revising *Auraicept na nEces,* 'The Scholar's Primer'. His poetry is quoted several times in *The Annals of the Four Masters* (FM 499, 507, 527 and 668). He was a descendant of Muirchertach mac Erca, and he was associated with Daire Lúrain (now Derryloran in Tyrone). His death is recorded in 679 in the annals (FM 677). See Edward O'Reilly, *A Chronological Account of nearly Four Hundred Irish Writers* (1820; rept. ed., New York, 1970), pp. 46-48, and John O'Donovan, ed. and trans., *Annala Ríoghachta Eireann, Annals of the Kingdom of Ireland by the Four Masters,* 7 vols. (1848-51; rept. ed., New York, 1966), vol. 1, pp. 161, 286.

32 The sentences of this paragraph appear in a slightly different order in the manuscript.

33 The titles on pages 53, 61, and 63 are not found in the manuscript. Frequently, however, long tales are composed of episodes which are given discrete names in the tale lists or in the texts of the stories themselves. I have used two of the later titles for the story of Cu-Chulainn's death to mark out the relevant episodes within this version of the tale. I have supplied 'The Victorious Onslaughts of Liath Macha' because of the suggestion in the text (p. 61) that the episode had a certain independent, proverbial fame.

34 The rivalry between CuChulainn and Conall (and a third hero, Loegaire) is the theme of *The Feast of Bricriu.*

35 Through the very act of speaking this poem, Conall

seems to discover that CuChulainn is dead and that Lugaid is the slayer. The incident provides an example of the way poetic utterance acts as a form of prophecy or revelation.

Textual notes: 'no yoke guides him', literally plural (reading *cumgit*), 'yokes do not guide him'; 'wrecked chariot' translates *fonnaide* which denotes some part of a chariot, possibly the wheel-rim or tyre, making the line an example of synecdoche.

36 Usually Ulster heroes ride in chariots, a trait which is part of the Iron-Age setting of the cycle (see Kenneth Jackson, *The Oldest Irish Tradition: A Window on the Iron Age*, Cambridge, 1964). Here, however, Conall is a *marcach*, one mounted on a horse; this is a later cultural element in the story.

37 Heroism was associated with heat: the greater a hero, the more heated he was believed to be. This episode turns on those beliefs. See above, also, p.38 and the references cited in note 2, where the same ideas occur.

38 Lugaid's claim has a legal dimension to it: Conall's vengeance for CuChulainn will not be adequate unless Lugaid is killed in his home territory.

39 *Belach Gabráin*, 'Gabran roadway', was a famous passage between Leinster and Ossairge; Sliab Mairge also stands on the border between Leinster and Ossairge (Hogan, *Onomasticon*, pp. 101, 610).

40 Conall's reply defines his own legal obligations in the situation. Normally he would be responsible for beasts and legal minors under his care, but this was not specified in his promise to Lugaid.

41 In the manuscript this title is found in the midst of the prophetic poem, after the first stanza.

42 Literally 'like a dead man'. It is a common folk belief in Ireland and elsewhere that the spirit of a person who has died by foul play will become a restless ghost, often to roam or ride about until the perpetrators of the crime are discovered and punished.

43 'Dechtire's dog' is probably an allusion to CuChulainn whose name means 'the dog (hound) of Culann'. The reference to placing fair treasures on CuChulainn is curious in the context of instructions about burial rites. Perhaps it is an allusion to burial customs in

101

which the valuables of a hero or other important person were placed in the grave along with his body.

44 Eithniu's son is the Celtic god Lug, CuChulainn's father. When CuChulainn is outnumbered and weary in *Táin Bó Cúailnge*, Lug comes to heal and aid him until CuChulainn recovers (Kinsella, *The Táin*, pp. 142-47). The theme of the stanza fits the Christian message of the poem: Lug's protection is not powerful enough to avert disaster.

45 *Textual notes* to 'CuChulainn's Ghostly Prophetic-Words'. S. 1: 'Patrick's lifetime', literally 'the time of Talcend' ('the adze-head', a nickname for Patrick); 'will come to you . . . a holy one', emending *dobním* to *dúib nóib*; Succet is Patrick's baptismal name; 'Heaven's high king', literally 'the king of high Heaven'; 'farewell till we meet again, Emain', literally 'that [be] good till we meet again, Emain'. S. 2: 'for Loeg I crushed men', reading the verb as 1 sg., but perhaps 'your favourite crushed men'. S. 3: 'I will attack many men like a murdered man', probably should read *dofías mór fer mart* (taking *mar fer* as a case of dittography), 'I will attack many dead men', which would be repeated by the last line of this stanza and hence give a perfect closing to this section of the poem; 'a splendid fine time', reading *ainré*; 'on Dechtire's dog', *cú* is the short dative in place of the usual *coin*; 'a heroic chariot-fighter, a noble god', the order of these clauses has been reversed and a verb has been omitted (literally 'should a heroic chariot-fighter arrive'). S. 4: 'I called upon', in the original the tense and person of the verb form are obscure; 'consider, Conall', emending *Conall* to the vocative; 'from salmon-plain to heart-plain', literally 'from Mag Eo to Mag Cride', *eó* is actually g. pl. of *eó* 'shaft, tree, yew', but a play of words on *eó* 'salmon' seems to fit the context.

46 *Textual notes* to 'CuChulainn's prophecy of the coming of Christ'. S. 1: 'in the beginning Christ lifted up the lands', literally 'Christ received (took) the lands first'; 'in return for Adam's shame', reading *i n-écrib* from *éric* 'payment, compensation'. S. 2: 'the King will heal the earth', or 'the King will redeem the earth'. S. 3: 'as One, as Two, as Three', literally 'by

102

ones, by twos, by threes'; 'which you do not brush aside / nor approve, nor oppose', the verb forms in these lines are difficult to analyze but they seem to have legal usages related to proceedings a plaintiff might initiate; 'will be long absent', literally 'a long absence'; 'the moon will swell', the verb presents difficulties, perhaps to be read as 3 sg. pret. of a compound of *lethaid* 'spreads out' S. 4: 'Jesus, most noble, most humble one', literally 'Jesus who is higher, who is lower', the phrase follows 'by dying' in the manuscript; 'by dying', literally 'by his funeral', could also be translated 'by his service' or 'by his visit'; 'over firmament / over men, over creatures' could also be translated 'over Heaven / over Man, over Creation', *dúil* 'creatures' or 'Creation' can also refer to the four elements.

47   In the manuscript the title is found directly before the poem.

48   Umendruad's name occurs in a pedigree in LL 107a30, 'Cu Chulaind mac Sualtaim meic Becaltaig meic Moraltaig meic Umendrúaid a sídib. & Dolb mac Becaltaig a brathair. & Ethne Ingubai ben Elcmaire a sídib. a síur'. In this tradition CuChulainn's father, Sualtaim, is from the otherworld; and Umendruad is an otherworldly ancestor of CuChulainn.

The reading of the text here should be *meic hUmendrúaid* instead of *meic hui Nendrúaid* as LL is presently edited.

Here in the poem Umendruad's descendants are credited with contributing to CuChulainn's achievements and success. Clearly this passage is related to the section in the Stowe version of *Táin Bó Cúailnge* where Dolb and Indolb come from the *síd* to help CuChulainn against FerDiad (see Cecile O'Rahilly, ed., *The Stowe Version of Táin Bó Cuailnge* [Dublin, 1961], ll. 3160-90).

49   This stanza is rich in allusions. The reference to Cu-Chulainn's death occurring on Wednesday is related to a tradition of assigning heroes' deaths to specific days of the week. A poem in this tradition is attributed to Flannacán mac Cellaich (d. 896) and preserved in In it each day of the week is associated with a list of

103

the heroes who were believed to have died on that day (Thurneysen, *Heldensage*, p. 19).

The passage also indicates that CuChulainn died at Lugnasad, the festival marking the beginning of harvest season. It may be more than fortuitous in this regard that hags play such a large role in CuChulainn's destruction. The figure of the hag — with various symbolic associations — appears over and over in Lugnasad legends (see MacNeill, *Festival of Lughnasa*, passim).

50 Emer's lament focuses here on her own worldly losses, a traditional element in Celtic elegy. Women and poets in particular are portrayed lamenting in this fashion. This section of the poem is reminiscent of lines in the Irish laments attributed to Gormlaith who mourns her dead husband(s) (Osborn Bergin, ed. and trans., *Irish Bardic Poetry* [Dublin, 1970], pp. 202-15, 308-15). They also call to mind lines in the Welsh poems set in the mouth of the character Heledd who mourns for her dead brother Cynddylan (e.g., Anthony Conran, trans., *The Penguin Book of Welsh Verse* [Harmondsworth, 1967], pp. 90-91).

'Honours', *míad*, could also be translated 'dignities, rank, status'; 'giving', *gart*, refers specifically to 'hospitality, generosity, honourable behaviour', along with valour a main quality in a chief or warrior (*Contributions*, 'G', cols. 47-48); 'rank', *grád*, might also be read 'love'; 'deeds' is literally singular.

51 'An improper course', *éccóir*, is literally 'a wong, impropriety, injustice'. The word is used both of errors of judgment and of moral wrong (*DIL*, 'E', col. 17). In early Irish sagas a king's error of judgment (usually in a somewhat restricted, legal sense) could cause crops to fail or could lead ultimately to the loss of the kingship (e.g., Kinsella, *The Táin*, p.4; Whitley Stokes, ed. and trans., 'The Battle of Mag Mucrime', *Revue celtique* 13 [1892], 460-63; cf. *Compert Cormaic*, 'The Birth of Cormac', ed. and trans., Standish H. O'Grady, *Silva Gadelica*, 2 vols. [London, 1892], vol. 1, pp. 253-56; vol. 2, pp. 286-89). Possibly the notion that CuChulainn's death results from an error in judgment is related to this motif. However, the

passage may simply suggest a broad concept of heroic mistake or fault. Cf. above, pp. 12-14 and note 1 to the Introduction.

52 *Textual notes* to 'Emer's Loud Lament', part one. S. 1: 'to see you', the text is corrupt, perhaps should read *dondat-éccai* 'to him who sees you'; 'with soothing words', literally 'with an abundance of consolations'; 'over your left side', or perhaps 'over your body'. S. 2: 'if he found sorrows', 'if' is supplied. S. 3: 'that slashed / enemies', literally 'when it slashed enemies'. S. 4: 'took heed of me' or 'cared for me'. S. 5: 'singular slaughter' could also be read as gen. pl. ('single combats'), a reading which suggests a variant of the story emphasizing CuChulainn's slaughter of the host (cf. n. 13, above); 'he died', reading *at-mbebai*, but possibly 3 sg. future (*Contributions, 'A'*, col. 444); 'hags crushed', literally 'hags ruined (spoiled)'; 'foul faces of female powers', literally 'faces of ugly *geniti*', *geniti* are female beings of malevolent powers (*Contributions, 'G'*, col. 69); 'brought to oblivion', reading the verb as a denominative verb formed from *díchuimne* forgetfulness, oblivion'. S. 6: 'whom Time snatched', *ré* 'Time' is a period of time in general and specifically the length of time a person lives, a lifetime; 'he went off pierced', the translation is tentative reading *tollus* 'perforation'; 'his strength overflowed', the verb is obscure, perhaps to be read in connection with *tethra* 'sea'?; 'a great snare', the noun is obscure, reading *tindell* (**to-indell*) 'a snare, plot, treachery' or perhaps *dindell* 'cancelling'; 'to hold', reading *cossecht* tentatively as an elsewhere unattested verbal noun in 't' of *con-secha* 'restrains, holds back'; 'the warrior was half-dead', literally 'his half-warrior was dead'.

53 I have reordered this run so that the clauses are in numerical order. There are similar runs in other sagas of the Ulster cycle (e.g. Kinsella, *The Táin*, pp. 155-56, 239). Using this convention a story-teller could quickly suggest great numbers of slain people while retaining the concrete, personal dimension of a list of individual names.

54 In a poem in *The Sick-Bed of CuChulainn* Emer also reproaches the Ulstermen for failing to aid CuChulainn

— there for failing to find a cure for his wasting sickness. That poem and the one here are related by their theme and their litanylike structure (cf. *Ancient Irish Tales,* pp. 185-86).

55 The reference to MesGegra here is very unusual and obscure. Mesgegra's death is recounted in *Talland Etair,* 'The Siege of Howth' (ed. and trans. Whitley Stokes, 'The Siege of Howth', *Revue celtique* 8 [1887], 47-64). There MesGegra is killed by Conall Cernach in revenge for his brothers MesDead and Loegaire. Conall Cernach's battle with MesGegra is similar to his battle with Lugaid in *The Death of CuChulainn:* MesGegra is one-handed; Conall fights him with one hand tied to his side; MesGegra's head is carried off; and venom from it perforates a stone. There are even similarities in the dialogue in the two sagas. In *The Siege of Howth* Conall eventually carries off only MesGegra's brain-ball because the head is too heavy. Later in *Aided Conchobuir,* 'The Death of Conchobor', MesGegra's brain-ball is captured by Cet mac Magach and used to maim Conchobor: the brain-ball is cast into Conchobor's head, lodges there, and ultimately causes his death. MesGegra is, thus, a very fateful person.

   Is it possible that Conall's fight with Lugaid in *The Death of CuChulainn* has been modelled on his fight with MesGegra, or is the opposite more likely? How are we to interpret Emer's reference to MesGegra? Could there once have been a version of CuChulainn's death that somehow involved MesGegra?

56 This seems to be an allusion to a version of the saga in which Cormac aided Conall in avenging CuChulainn's death.

57 The poem alludes here to *The Wooing of Emer.* In this context perhaps the 'woman of the *síd*' might be identified with Aife whom CuChulainn overcame and impregnated. However, if *breth,* translated 'carrying off', is translated 'judgment' ('after the judgment of a woman of the *síd*'), the line might be construed as an allusion to Scathach who trained CuChulainn in arms, judged him fit as a fighter, and delivered a prophetic utterance about the course of his life (see Kinsella, *The Táin,* pp. 29-37).

106

58 *Textual notes* to 'Emer's Loud Lament', part two. S. 1: 'grief! / red-bladed Feidlimid', in the original this line like the last begins 'misery!', apparently indicating that a line beginning 'grief!' has been lost; hereafter in ss. 1 and 2 'grief!' and 'misery!' are inverted; 'did not watch over him', reading the verb as a form of *for-aicci* 'surveys'; 'that all Ulster's heroes were not', literally 'that Ulster's heroes were not together'. S. 2: 'that all Ulster was not', literally 'that the Ulstermen were not together'. S. 3: 'his death has made me weak', literally 'his dying without male issue', the word *díbad* implies that an inheritance line is becoming extinct and gives resonance to the word 'barren (fruitless)' in the next line. S. 4: 'each eye that saw him', the word for eye is *rosc,* the poetic eye associated with visionary power, second sight, prophecy and poetry. S. 6: 'MesGegra of many deeds / has perished', reading *gnímrathae*; 'he got away with treachery', reading *luing* from *lang* 'treachery'; 'he struck swiftly', taking the verb from *sáidid* 'thrusts', but if *sad* can be read as 'greyhound' (cf. Stokes, 'Eulogy', p. 3, note 36), perhaps 'he escaped by treachery / a swift dog of terrible deeds' (an allusion to CuChulainn?). S. 7: 'a woman of the *síd*', reading *ban-síde* with *ban-* as the composition form of *ben*; 'with the trophy of a torque . . . he drove about', literally 'he drove about with the trophy of a (wheel)', the word *roth* can be used of many wheel-shaped things including chariot-wheels and wheel-brooches, possibly the line is metonymy for 'chariot'; 'and banished', reading *echtraid* 'banishes'. S. 8: 'say that I knew', reading *ro-fessur.* S. 9: 'the shadowy tribes', reading *mor-* (cf. the discussion of *Morrígan, Contributions, 'M',* col. 173); 'and peoples', supplied for the sake of lineation.

BIBLIOGRAPHY

THE DEATH OF CU ROI

Editions

R. I. Best, ed. and trans., 'The Tragic Death of CúRói
Mac Dári', *Eriu* 2 (1905), 18-35.

Whitley Stokes, ed., 'The Eulogy of CúRói, Amra Chonrói',
Eriu 2 (1905), 1-14.

Other Versions

Kuno Meyer, ed., 'Addenda to M. de Jubainville's *Catalogue
de la littérature épique de l'Irlande'*, *Revue celtique* 6
(1884), 187-91. Laud 610.

Kuno Meyer, ed. and trans., 'Brinna Ferchertne', *Zeitschrift für celtische Philologie* 3 (1899), 40-46.

Rudolf Thurneysen, 'Die Sage von CuRoi', *Zeitschrift
für celtische Philologie* 9 (1913), 189-234. Egerton
88; versions of the *dindshenchas* story of Finnglais
from LL and the Book of Ballymote.

THE DEATH OF CU CHULAINN

Editions

R. I. Best, O. J. Bergin, and M. A. O'Brien, eds., *The Book
of Leinster, formerly Lebar na Núachongbála*, 5 vols.,
(Dublin, 1954-   ). The text of *Aided ConCulainn* is
found in vol. 2, pp. 442-57.

Rudolf Thurneysen, *Zu irischen Handschriften und Littera-
turdenkmälern*, Zweite Serie (Berlin, 1913) (*Abhand-
lungen der königlichen Gesellschaft der Wissenschaften
zu Göttingen*, Philologisch-historische Klasse, Neue
Folge, Band 14, no. 3). Variants from H.3.18 are
found on pp. 13-19.

Translations

Henri d'Arbois de Jubainville, ed., *L'Epopée celtique en
Irlande* (Paris, 1892), pp. 326-73.

Georges Dottin, *L'Epopée irlandaise* (Paris, 1926). Translation of *The Death of CuChulainn* appears on pp.

Christian-J. Guyonvarc'h, trans., 'La Mort de Cúchulainn, version A, texte traduit du moyen-irlandais', *Ogam* 18 (1966), 343-64.

Whitley Stokes, trans., 'CúChulainn's Death, Abridged from the Book of Leinster, ff. 77, a.1-78, b.2', *Revue celtique* 3 (1877), 175-85.

The Fifteenth-Century Version

A. G. VanHamel, ed., *Compert Con Culainn and Other Stories* (Dublin, 1956), pp. 69-133.

John Hogan and H. H. Lloyd, eds., 'Brisleach mhór Mhaighe Mhuirtheimhne', *Gaelic Journal* 11 (1901) and 17 (1907).

Christian-J. Guyonvarc'h, trans., 'La Mort de Cúchulainn', *Celticum* 7 (1962), 1-40.

Standish H. O'Grady, trans., 'The great defeat on the Plain of Muirthemne before Cuchullin's Death', in *The Cuchullin Saga in Irish Literature*, ed. Eleanor Hull (London, 1898), pp. 235-49.

GENERAL

Thomas Kinsella, trans., *The Táin: Translated from the Irish Epic Táin Bó Cúailnge* (1969; rept. ed., London and New York, 1970).

Tom Peete Cross and Clark Harris Slover, eds., *Ancient Irish tales* (1936; rept. ed., New York, 1969.

Josef Baudis, 'Cúrói and Cúchulainn', *Eriu* 7 (1914), 200-9.

Françoise Le Roux, 'La Mort de Cúchulainn, commentaire du texte', *Ogam* 18 (1966), 365-99.

Daniel F. Melia, 'Remarks on the Structure and Composition of the Ulster Death Tales', *Studia Hibernica* 17/18 (1977-78), 36-57.

Rudolf Thurneysen, *Die irische Helden- und Königsage bis zum siebzehnten Jahrhundert* (Halle, 1921).